Sunny

Rishelle.

Nick

ELMO

LIZ

EMILY RODDA'S
RAVEN HILL MYSTERIES

CASE #3: BEWARE THE GINGERBREAD HOUSE

Be on the lookout for all of
Emily Rodda's Raven Hill Mysteries:

EMILY RODDA'S
RAVEN HILL MYSTERIES

CASE #3: BEWARE THE GINGERBREAD HOUSE

Emily Rodda

SCHOLASTIC INC.

New York Toronto London Auckland Sydney
Mexico City New Delhi Hong Kong Buenos Aires

ISBN 0-439-78248-1

Series concept copyright © 1994 by Emily Rodda
Text copyright © 1994 by Scholastic Australia

All rights reserved. Published by Scholastic Inc., 557 Broadway, New York, NY 10012, by arrangement with Scholastic Press, an imprint of Scholastic Australia.

SCHOLASTIC, APPLE PAPERBACKS, and associated logos are trademarks and/or registered trademarks of Scholastic Inc.

12 11 10 9 8 7 6 5 4 3 2 1   5 6 7 8 9 10/0

Printed in the U.S.A.
First American edition, December 2005

EMILY RODDA'S
RAVEN HILL MYSTERIES

CASE #3: BEWARE THE GINGERBREAD HOUSE

Contents

1

No good reason

Dressing up as a rabbit to sell cakes isn't my idea of a sensible job. But Help-for-Hire Inc. has said yes to crazy jobs before, and I've never objected.

I guess that was why Liz, Tom, Elmo, Nick, and Richelle were so surprised when I said I didn't want to work at the Gingerbread House.

"I can't *understand* you, Sunny Chan," Liz shrieked. "You go along with all sorts of boring, yucky jobs when we're overloaded. And then a dream chance comes along just when we really need it, and you say no!"

She waved her hands at the kids streaming out of the school yard. "Don't you realize that there isn't a single person at Raven Hill High who wouldn't give an arm and a leg for this?"

"There is, as a matter of fact," I said. "Me."

Nick and Richelle looked at each other, and Richelle rolled her eyes. They didn't mean for me to see, of course, but I did. I stared at Richelle, and she just blinked at me lazily without smiling, and flicked back her long blond hair.

"I don't think I'd give an arm *and* a leg, actually," Tom said, with his face all screwed up as though he was really considering it.

"Oh, shut up, Tom!" shouted Liz. "This is serious. Without Sunny, we're a person short. Mrs. Crumb wants six rabbits. Six! And I told her we'd do it. I never dreamed anyone would object. Good money, a chance to show everyone how reliable we are again — and all that cake and stuff for free!"

Tom moaned softly to himself. He dug around in his pocket and found a half-eaten Snickers bar. It was a bit melted at one end, but he started chewing on it, anyway.

Liz put her hands on her hips and glared at me. "Sunny, as far as I know, you haven't even been *inside* the Gingerbread House," she said. "How do you know you won't like it?"

My heart thudded. "I have been in it," I said, pleased that my voice sounded as level as usual. "A year ago, when it first opened."

"Well, then you know it's fabulous. So give me *one* good reason why you don't want the job," Liz demanded.

I couldn't tell her the truth. I just couldn't. And none of them would have believed me if I did. So I took a breath, looked straight into Liz's worried hazel eyes, and lied.

"I'll give you three good reasons," I said firmly. "One, I don't want to dress up in some stupid rabbit costume. Two, my father's arriving from Australia tomorrow for the school vacation, and I want to spend some time with him. Three, I don't like cake."

"Well, *that's* not a problem," Tom put in cheerfully. "You can give your share of the goodies to me."

"If anyone thinks *I* want to wear one of those gross rabbit costumes, they're wrong," remarked Richelle, inspecting her fingernails with a frown. "Those big teeth! And the starey eyes! Yuck! And *I* certainly won't be eating lots of cake — everyone knows *I* don't eat fattening food. It's just that *I* happen to want Help-for-Hire Inc. to go on. *I* don't want to be selfish and let everyone else down."

"Besides, you owe your mother a fortune because of those boots you got, and you need the money," I couldn't help saying. I wasn't going to let Richelle get away with pretending to be unselfish for the first time in her life.

Liz sighed heavily.

At this point, Elmo decided it was time to move off the sidelines and do his part for peace. "If Sunny doesn't want the job, we could always get someone else to stand in for her," he said.

It was a sensible suggestion, but I knew Liz wouldn't go for it.

Sure enough, she frowned. "We can't do that!" she objected. "We're supposed to be a team. A reliable team. Once we start letting strange kids in, the whole point of Help-for-Hire Inc. will disappear. And now — especially now — we have to show everyone we're still a strong group."

She bit her lip and looked at me reproachfully. I knew what was behind that look. *Why are you doing this, Sunny?* she was thinking. *You're my best friend. You're always so calm and sensible. I've always been able to depend on you.*

I hated disappointing Liz. Our part-time job agency was her baby. She'd thought of it when we all needed to make some money. She'd gotten us organized enough to advertise as a group. She'd really worked hard to get us started.

And we'd all done well so far, too. Sure, we'd gotten into a bit of trouble along the way. A few of our jobs had gotten us mixed up in mysteries and adventures — a couple of them quite dangerous. But that was half the fun. I thought so, anyway, though Richelle was always complaining about it.

But now Help-for-Hire Inc. was in a different kind of trouble. Trouble that wasn't fun. And I knew this wasn't the time to back out of a good job. Especially when my real reason for not wanting to work in the Gingerbread House didn't make any sense at all.

"We'll lose the gig if we don't make up our minds soon," Nick's cool voice put in. "The Work Demons would jump at it. And there are six of them."

Elmo and Liz scowled ferociously at the very mention of the Work Demons — this other group from Raven Hill High who'd copied our Help-for-Hire idea and were going around everywhere trying to scoop up all the best jobs.

But it was the thought of losing all that free food at the Gingerbread House that sent Tom over the edge. He threw himself down on one knee and held up his hands to me. A group of girls walking past stared at him and giggled behind their hands.

"Sunny, we've been through thick and thin together," he wailed. "Mainly thin. I beg of you, don't fail us now. Come with us to the Gingerbread House. We need you to protect us from the wicked witch."

I ignored him, but it did no good. He just raised his voice to a sort of trembling scream. "Oh, and think of the big, fluffy muffins, and the cream puffs, and the little tiny meringues that melt in your mouth," he begged. "Not to mention the chocolate truffles. They don't want to fall into the greedy paws of the Work Demons, Sunny. They want us. They want *me*!"

"Tom, get up," I said severely. But I could feel my mouth starting to curve into a grin. I couldn't help it. Tom always makes me laugh.

"Everyone's staring at you, Tom," hissed Richelle, turning away and trying to look as though she didn't belong with us.

He took no notice. He could see that I was weakening. He dragged himself toward me, still on one knee, and started tugging at the hem of my shirt. He looked ridiculous.

I just stood there, feeling helpless. Liz was running her hands through her hair in frustration. Elmo was grinning all over his freckled face. Nick — Mr. Cool — was looking disgusted. Richelle was edging even farther away from the embarrassment. Everyone was staring at us.

Why am I doing this? I thought suddenly. *Why am I causing all this fuss? I'm being idiotic. Childish.*

Suddenly, the fight didn't seem worth it.

"Oh, all right!" I said, half laughing and half angry, batting Tom's clutching hand away. "I'll do it! Now are you satisfied?"

"Perfectly," said Tom. He clambered to his feet and brushed dirt and clinging leaves off his knees. He grinned around and fluttered his eyelashes at the others. "Say thank you to Super Tom," he said. "Super Tom has saved the day."

"You're an idiot, Moysten," sneered Nick.

"Takes one to know one, Kontellis," snapped Tom, his grin changing like lightning to a sulky scowl.

I left them to it and started walking off toward the gate. Their bickering really irritates me sometimes.

Liz ran to catch up with me. We walked together in silence for a moment, feeling a bit awkward.

"So you'll really do it?" she said at last.

I shrugged. "I said so, didn't I?"

She went quiet again. I felt bad. I was giving Liz a hard time, for no good reason.

No good reason. I repeated the words to myself and tried to get them into my head. *No good reason.*

I pulled myself together and nudged Liz's arm. "It's OK, Liz," I said, and made myself grin. "Don't worry about it."

"Sunny, the job's every day but only till two-thirty. You'll still have plenty of time to see your dad. He'll be here for a week, won't he?"

Then I felt really bad. My dad wasn't the problem, though I had to admit I was a bit anxious about seeing him. It had been two years since his last visit. The rabbit suit wasn't the problem. The cake wasn't the problem.

No, I was the problem. Because of this Gingerbread House thing, I was struggling with something I couldn't handle.

It was crazy. It was illogical. I couldn't even start to explain it.

All I knew was that when I went into the Gingerbread House for the first — and only — time, an awful feeling had settled over me.

First, though I knew I hadn't, I felt I'd seen the place before, a long time ago. I felt that I'd already faced those sugar-frosted windows and those candy-cane posts by the toffee-colored front door. And in my memory, evil and darkness were spilling out of that door, like a gas you couldn't see or smell.

Then the woman inside the shop had leaned over the counter and beckoned to me. She'd smiled, her long nose nearly meeting her pointed chin, and her big teeth glittering.

"What can I do for you, my pretty?" she cackled, fixing me with her pale eyes. "Come in. Come in."

I tried to talk, but I couldn't. My throat felt as though it had closed up. I started seeing double. My hands were slippery with sweat.

I couldn't understand it. At first, I thought I was sick. And then I realized, clutching my shopping bag and money, unable to move, that for no good reason I was feeling something I hadn't felt since I was very, very little.

I was scared. Scared to death.

2

The Gingerbread House

I never get scared. I get riled up when there's something important happening, like before a gymnastics meet or a tae kwon do test. And when something dangerous happens, I can feel my whole body start to tingle, ready for action.

But I don't seem to feel what other people call "scared." I don't know why. Liz, who's into psychology, says it's because I always concentrate on what has to be done to escape from danger, instead of imagining what might happen to me if I don't. Richelle says it's because I haven't got any nerves.

And I certainly don't believe in witches — or in magic, or ghosts, or astrology, or any of that sort of stuff. Everyone knows that.

Sometimes, Liz gets irritated with me because of it. "You can't just say *none* of it's true, Sunny!" she says to me. "The world's full of strange things we don't understand. You have to keep an open mind."

"Show me hard proof, and I'll believe anything," I always say.

So then she says I'm boring and have no imagination. Because, of course, she can't give me any proof. There's no proof to give.

Anyway, I guess that's why my spooked feeling about the Gingerbread House shocked me so much. Because for me, of all people, to be scared of a fake witch — well, it's just ridiculous.

✿

I thought it through over the weekend.

While Saturday morning went on as usual at our house — my mother seeing patients in her office at the front, my four older sisters and I doing housework at the back — I thought.

At Saturday afternoon gymnastics class, I thought.

Talking to Dad when he took Penny, Cathy, Amy, Sarah, and me to dinner that night, I thought.

At our Sunday lunch with Mom's grandmother, listening to her complaints about our wicked Western ways in general and my father in particular, and eating the best Chinese food in the history of the world, I thought.

On Sunday night, lying in bed in the room I share with Cathy, I thought.

And as I walked to the Raven Hill Mall on Monday morning to meet the others, I reminded myself of what I'd worked out.

I reminded myself that whatever stupid thing I'd felt when I first visited the Gingerbread House, it was only a pastry shop, after all. Even if it *was* decorated to look like something out of a fairy tale. And I told myself that Hazel Crumb, the owner, was just an ordinary woman. An ordinary woman, and a very good cook, who had a business to run.

It wasn't her fault that her nose was long and hooked. Or that her chin was sharp and jutted out. It didn't matter that she always wore black. Or that when she smiled, as she did all the time, her big teeth glittered, but her pale eyes seemed to stay as still and cold as river stones.

If she looked like a witch, that only made her shop more successful. Everyone in Raven Hill knew Hazel Crumb and the Gingerbread House.

Everyone, little kids especially, loved the way the shop looked just like the witch's cottage in "Hansel and Gretel." Of course, it wasn't really made of gingerbread, sugar, and chocolate, like the house in the fairy tale. It had just been built and painted to look that way. But it had been done so well that you really felt as though you could break off a piece of the roof to eat, or lick the windows and taste sugar.

And, of course, the little kids adored it when Mrs. Crumb beckoned them in, smiling her witch-smile and cackling as they crept through the fancy door, pretending to be scared.

They'd whisper and giggle to one another as they stood in front of the counter that looked like chocolate, while their mothers and fathers bought cakes and muffins. They'd stare with hungry eyes at the big glass jars on the shelves behind the counter.

Every jar was crammed with a different kind of candy. There were jelly beans of every flavor, licorice, Gummi Bears, toffees, peppermints — absolutely everything you can think of. The Raven Hill dentist probably made millions off of the Gingerbread House.

Then the kids would peep through their fingers at the two little stools sitting in one corner of the shop, near the kitchen.

One stool was labeled "Hansel" and the other "Gretel." The kids knew that if they went and sat down on one of those stools, and the shop wasn't too busy, it was quite likely that Hazel Crumb would pounce out from behind the counter and slide her famous barred gate across the corner, trapping them in a cage.

Then she'd pretend to padlock the gate, and cackle at them in a witchy way, while their parents smiled and thought how cute they were. Everyone had a delicious, scary time.

At some time or another, after they'd nagged long and hard enough, most of the little kids who visited the Gingerbread House would end up being photographed in the cage, sticking a finger through the bars. Just like Hansel had had to do when the witch was trying to fatten him up to eat.

Mrs. Crumb herself took the photographs. She charged a lot for them, of course. Why else did she keep the stools and the gate there? And a Polaroid camera handy?

And that, I told myself as I jogged in through the mall entrance, *is what I have to remember most of all. It's all a matter of money.*

The whole witch thing was an act. A moneymaking act by a clever woman who was using her skill as a cook, and even her looks, to make an ordinary pastry shop into something special. It was that simple.

I headed for the escalator that would take me to the first floor. There was hardly anyone around. It was very early.

I took a breath and told myself how stupid I'd been a year ago, to be spooked by a fake. I was just lucky that none of the others had caught on to what was bothering me. I'd never have lived it down.

Anyway, I had it all worked out now. Didn't I?

Why then, as I reached the first floor, did my heart begin to sink down to my shoes? Why, when I saw the gleaming windows of the Gingerbread House, its fake frosted roof, its fake toffee front door firmly closed, did it jump back up into my mouth?

Because I'm crazy, that's why, I thought. Crazy. I must have been working too hard. I wasn't four years old. I didn't believe in witches. There was no reason for this. No reason . . .

"Sunny!"

Tom was waving to me, his long, skinny arm held up high. And there were Liz, Elmo, and Nick — all looking ordinary and happy, standing there waiting by the INFORMATION sign in the center of the tiled plaza.

I strolled up to them, trying to look as casual as always.

"Where's the wicked witch?" I heard myself saying.

"Richelle?" grinned Tom. "Late as usual."

"To-om!" Liz scolded him. She turned to me. "The shop doesn't open till eight-thirty. But the shutters are off the front windows. Mrs. Crumb must be in the kitchen at the back, baking."

Tom sniffed and sighed. "You can smell it," he said.

Sure enough, a delicious aroma was wafting in our direction. I swallowed, trying to control the shaking in my legs.

"Let's go in," said Nick. He always hated waiting around.

We walked toward the Gingerbread House. Liz glanced at me and frowned slightly. I had a feeling that my casual act hadn't fooled her.

I worked on keeping my face and voice as calm as I could, while my heart thudded so loudly you'd have thought that everyone would hear it.

"How's your father, Sunny?" Liz murmured to me. She'd probably decided that I was being weird because of Dad.

"He's fine," I said.

"Is he playing tennis while he's here?" she asked, keeping the conversation going.

I shook my head. "He's on vacation," I said. "No tennis coaching. No tennis. So far, anyway."

"When are you seeing him next?"

I shrugged. "He's supposed to be coming to watch my gymnastics class this afternoon, so I'll see him then, I guess. If he turns up. You never know with Dad."

I realized I'd said too much when I caught Liz's sympathetic look. I didn't want her, or anyone else, to feel sorry for me. After all, I didn't feel sorry for myself.

And why should I? I thought. My mother and sisters and I get along fine without Dad.

I'm the youngest in the family, and I was only four when he left and went to Australia to live.

Mom and the others have always said that I was his favorite, and followed him around everywhere. It was Dad who started calling me Sunny instead of Alice, my real name. And I adored him in those days, apparently.

But I don't remember all that, and I don't miss him. Not like Tom, who really does miss his father, though he sees him often.

Dad hardly ever visits. I've seen his photograph in magazines and newspapers much more than I've seen him in person. But so what? Roy Chan, ex-international tennis champion, now a glamorous tennis coach, is just a laughing stranger with a slight Australian accent and a famous face — to me at least.

But I could see that Liz was worrying about me, and I was irritated. Not with her. She's as soft as butter, and she cares about me. Who could be irritated about that? But I was angry with myself, for dropping my guard and letting her even *think* I had a problem.

We were almost at the door of the Gingerbread House when there was a cackle of laughter from inside. Mrs. Crumb was in there all right. But by the sound of it, she wasn't alone.

"You're very persuasive, boys," she said. Her voice reached us clearly. She must have been standing right beside the door.

"So what d'you say?" said another voice. It was a voice we knew. Unfortunately.

We looked at one another. Tom opened his mouth, but Nick held up a furious hand, and he kept quiet.

Mrs. Crumb laughed again. "I think I'll stick with the team I've got, thanks, Darren," she said. "They're cheaper than you are, for a start."

"That's what Burger Joe said when he took them on instead of us," said the first voice. "But like we told you, he regretted it."

Elmo muttered something under his breath. Liz flushed bright red. I could feel my fists clenching with rage. The Work Demons were in there. Or at least Darren Henshaw, the leader of the gang, was. Trying to steal our job.

3

Hazel Crumb

"Well, I'll take my chances," said Mrs. Crumb. "Now, you'd better skedaddle. They'll be here soon, and they won't be too happy to find you here."

There were loud guffaws. The Work Demons seemed to find that very funny.

My fingers tingled. I looked sideways at Elmo and Liz. They looked like thunderclouds about to rumble.

The door opened. We stepped back as Darren Henshaw, Nutley Frean, and the rest of the Work Demon uglies swaggered out.

Darren smirked, running his fingers through his thick black hair. "Well, well, it's the cockroach kids."

"Why don't you do the world a favor and get lost, Henshaw?" said Tom.

Darren charged up to him and grabbed him by the shirt. Tom is taller than he is, but much skinnier. We all knew that Darren could beat him to a pulp if he wanted to.

"That's enough, thank you," snapped Mrs. Crumb from

the doorway. "You boys just move along. I don't want any trouble here."

Darren went on holding a fistful of Tom's shirt for just long enough to show that he meant business. Then he let go, giving Tom a hard little jab in the chest as he did it.

"Sure you don't want to change your mind?" he said to Mrs. Crumb.

"Positive," she answered firmly.

"Yay, Mrs. Crumb," murmured Tom under his breath. He was looking a bit white and rubbing at his chest. Darren's knuckles had probably given him a bad bruise. But you couldn't keep Tom down.

Darren curled his lip. "Suit yourself."

He jerked his head at his grinning friends, and they started to move along, pushing roughly past us.

"Come inside," Mrs. Crumb said, gesturing toward us.

We crowded forward. I went with the rest. But suddenly, with the sight of her beckoning, bony fingers, all the fear I'd forgotten during the Work Demons drama had come rushing back.

"Hey!"

We spun around at the shout. Darren, Nutley, and the others were standing near the INFORMATION sign.

"You'll be so-orry!" they all shouted. Then they screamed with laughter and made for the escalator, shoving and scuffling with one another.

We watched till they disappeared from sight.

"What do you think they meant by that?" demanded Nick.

I shrugged.

"Who cares?" I said. But as I followed him into the Gingerbread House, I wondered. What *had* the Work Demons meant?

Was Mrs. Crumb going to be sorry she'd given us this job?

Or were we the ones who would be sorry?

❁

"So . . . my little rabbits," began Mrs. Crumb, smiling her scary, toothy smile. Then she frowned. "But there are only five of you!" she exclaimed.

Liz opened her mouth to explain, but exactly at that moment, the door opened again and Richelle slipped in, pink-cheeked and wide-eyed.

She looked like something out of a fairy tale herself. Like one of those princesses who are always getting locked in towers and having to be rescued. I think she must have done it purposely. She was wearing a soft, floaty dress that exactly matched her big blue eyes, and her long blond hair was sort of tumbling around her shoulders in golden waves.

"Sorry I'm late," she breathed, fluffing up her hair and fluttering her eyelashes at Mrs. Crumb. "I've been in such a *panic*. My father had trouble with the car."

"Oh, no," exclaimed Tom. "Don't tell me you had to *walk*? Like the rest of us peasants?"

Richelle tilted her head to one side. "No," she said. "I had to wait. That's why I'm late."

"Well, you're here now, dear," said Mrs. Crumb warmly. Like

17

most adults, she seemed very impressed by Richelle. At least it proved that, despite her witchy appearance, she was no different from anyone else.

"Mrs. Crumb," Liz began awkwardly. "About Burger Joe's . . ."

But Mrs. Crumb waved her hand. "Don't worry," she said. "Darren Henshaw told me nothing I didn't already know. Word travels fast in the mall, Liz."

"And you gave us the job, anyway?" Liz was pink with embarrassment.

Mrs. Crumb cackled, stretching her mouth wide. "I'm not hiring you to clean the place, right?" she said. "Fortunately."

Liz hesitated and glanced at me. I knew she wanted me to say something, but I couldn't. Nick decided to fill in the gap.

"There wasn't a single dead cockroach in the kitchen when we left Burger Joe's that night, Mrs. Crumb," he said firmly. "There was no dirty oil on the benches. The place was completely clean. And there was no bad hamburger meat in the refrigerator, either, as far as we know."

"Didn't smell like it, anyway," Tom put in bluntly.

"Is that so?" said Mrs. Crumb, her cold eyes fixed on him. "Yet I gather that at seven-thirty the next morning, when the health inspectors came, the place was far from . . . uh . . . attractive."

"Someone must have broken in and messed up the place overnight," Nick said. "Someone who wanted Burger Joe's closed down."

Mrs. Crumb's eyebrows rose, and the corner of her mouth twitched. You could tell she thought this was very unlikely.

"It was so *infuriating*," Richelle burst out. "I just about *ruined* my nails, scrubbing. And then for people to say those benches were oily and dirty — well, *honestly!*"

We, of course, had heard this complaint from Richelle before. About a thousand times, as a matter of fact. But Mrs. Crumb looked at Richelle sharply, and with some surprise. Then she rubbed her pointed chin, frowning thoughtfully. "I see," she murmured. "Well, well."

I suddenly realized that Richelle had succeeded where Liz, Nick, and Tom had failed. She'd convinced Mrs. Crumb that we really had cleaned Burger Joe's very carefully that night.

I guess it was because Richelle was so obviously really upset. Not because poor Joe's place had been closed down. Not because Help-for-Hire's reputation for being a resourceful, reliable work team had been shattered. But because her beautiful nails had been damaged for nothing.

She was inspecting them now, sighing heavily.

Mrs. Crumb, still frowning, abruptly turned and went to the swinging door that led to the kitchen.

"Your costumes are in the storeroom back here," she said shortly, pushing the door open.

"What's the matter with her?" Nick muttered.

I wondered, too. Mrs. Crumb had seemed happier when she thought we'd left Burger Joe's shop a mess of oil and cockroaches.

"She's probably angry for poor Joe," Liz whispered back.

"If she cared about him, she wouldn't have hired us in the first place," Elmo said as we followed Mrs. Crumb into the warm kitchen. "No one else in the mall would touch us, would they?"

"She's just weird," yawned Richelle. "Everyone says so."

Liz frowned. But for once, I agreed with Richelle.

In the kitchen, a plump, red-faced girl in a huge white apron was standing at a workbench loading cupcakes from a cooling rack onto a tray.

"Hi," she said, turning around and grinning at us. "I'm Julie."

Mrs. Crumb went into a small room set into the kitchen wall beside two huge ovens. We heard her rummaging in there. When she reappeared, she was smiling again. Two limp, furry bodies trailed over one of her arms, their arms flopping, their legs trailing on the floor. In one hand she held up a grinning rabbit head. Its bright blue eyes were fixed and mad-looking. Its ears were lined with furry pink silky stuff.

She beckoned with her free hand. "Come along, children," she called, and cackled with laughter.

My heart thumped violently in my chest. A wave of dark fear washed over me, blotting out all thought, turning my legs to jelly.

No! a voice in my head screamed out. *No! Get out! Get out!*

But Tom was pushing me from behind, and Liz was nudging at my arm.

There was no way out.

4

My life as a rabbit

Afterward, when Mrs. Crumb had gone back to work and we were struggling into our crazy rabbit suits, I wondered what I'd been going on about. Again the panic had died down, leaving me feeling trembly and stupid.

No one noticed how quiet I was. Everyone was too busy laughing and messing around.

Finally, a heavy paw tapped me on the shoulder. "What's up, Doc?" said Tom's voice, muffled by his suit.

I had to smile. It was really funny to see this enormous rabbit looming over me. Tom was already tall, and the rabbit head made him even taller.

I was another matter. I am the shortest person in the group, and even though they'd given me the smallest suit, it still swam on me. The legs and arms fell in fat, furry folds around my ankles and wrists. It was pretty uncomfortable, I can tell you. And I could hardly move.

"You're a saggy, baggy rabbit, Sunny," said Elmo, making one of his rare jokes.

"I think she looks cute," said Liz, poking at me with safety pins.

She pinned me up as best she could. Then we put on our rabbit heads.

The head rested on my shoulders and was heavier than it looked. There was a patch of stiff wire netting in the neck, just opposite my eyes and nose. That's how people wearing these suits can see and breathe. The rabbit face sat up much higher. No wonder everyone looked so tall.

We stood there laughing at one another.

"This is classic. I should have brought my camera," said a voice. I knew it must be Nick, but looking around at the identical white rabbits in front of me, I couldn't tell which one he was.

"Haw, haw, haw!" bellowed a voice. "Hey, Mrs. Crumb, take a look at this!"

It was Julie, holding a huge tray of cinnamon buns in her strong arms and grinning all over her face.

"All right, Julie, settle down," called Mrs. Crumb. "And keep going. It's eight-fifteen. We're late." She came over to where we were standing, scanned us all, and nodded with satisfaction.

"Very good," she said. "Excellent. Now . . ."

She was carrying two big cheesecakes that had been decorated with cream and blueberries. She put them down on the counter and hurried away. I heard the tall rabbit next to me growl hungrily under its breath. Tom, I figured, grinning behind the shelter of my costume head.

One of the other rabbits was looking in a mirror hanging inside the storeroom door and smoothing its whiskers. That was Richelle, for sure.

And the rabbit that was anxiously brushing down the back of another's fur was probably Liz. Brushing Elmo down. Elmo always got his clothes messy. The one standing by itself, leaning against the wall, was certainly Nick. Trying to look cool even in a white rabbit suit.

Still, it was fascinating that only by these tiny clues could I even begin to tell one person from another. They were all in disguise. Except for me, of course, I realized. Being so saggy and baggy, I must have been quite recognizable to the rest of them.

Mrs. Crumb came back with a huge stack of leaflets advertising the Gingerbread House. She gave us each a bundle, and a pink cotton shoulder bag to put them in.

"I want these handed out all over the mall," Mrs. Crumb instructed.

We all nodded. Julie, thumping past with a tray of chocolate éclairs, guffawed loudly. "You couldn't look sillier," she said.

"Off you go, now," said Mrs. Crumb, ignoring her. "You can take a break at eleven, have something to eat and drink, and get more leaflets then. Use the back door. There's a Staff Only passage leading to it. Near the public bathroom at the end of this row of shops, you know?"

We nodded again.

"Oh, and Richelle? Which one of you is Richelle?"

The rabbit at the mirror put up a paw. *So I was right*, I thought with satisfaction.

"I have a bit of a problem tomorrow morning, Richelle," Mrs. Crumb was saying. "I have to cook for some orders, but I think we'll need two people to serve in the shop. There are some busloads of tourists coming to visit Exclusive Opals across the

23

plaza. They're likely to drift over here afterward. Would you be willing to help Julie serve?"

"Dressed like this?" asked Richelle.

Mrs. Crumb stared at her for a minute.

"No, she's not joking, Mrs. Crumb," muttered Tom's voice from somewhere in the mass of white fur around me. "I know it's hard to believe, but —"

The voice broke off abruptly. I guess someone had punched him.

"Well, no, Richelle," Mrs. Crumb said at last. "You couldn't really serve in the shop wearing the suit. It's much too clumsy."

"Oh, good," said Richelle. "I'll do it, then."

Mrs. Crumb looked pleased. *How strange*, I thought.

Mrs. Crumb was very clever in lots of ways. She organized the Gingerbread House well, and seemed to make plenty of money from it. She was popular with the customers. She got good ideas, like the rabbit team, to advertise her business.

But when it came to the people she got to work for her, she wasn't such a good judge. Julie was hardworking and cheery, but obviously not too bright. And now Mrs. Crumb had chosen Richelle, of all people, to serve in the shop tomorrow.

I would have thought anyone could see that Richelle was the most oblivious, most unreliable person in our group. I'm not being catty. Just realistic. Richelle's really only in Help-for-Hire Inc. because she's an old friend of Liz's. But even Liz can't cope with her sometimes. And, frankly, she drives me crazy.

"All right," said Mrs. Crumb briskly. "Off you go now!"

And so, with Julie's laughter echoing in our ears, we all

trailed to the front door and went out into the plaza to start our careers as white rabbits.

○

Most of the shops were open now, and there were quite a few people around. They stared, smiled, and pointed as we waddled across the plaza, getting used to moving in our clumsy suits. I was having a bit of trouble because of all my sags and bags. Liz's safety pins hadn't quite solved the problem.

"Isn't it strange?" Liz murmured beside me. "People can't see us, but we can see them."

"Of course, they can see us, Liz," snapped Richelle.

"They could hardly miss us," said Nick drily.

"I mean they can't see what we really look like," Liz retorted. "They can't tell who we are."

"So we're free!" squeaked Tom. He jumped up and down and waved his arms. A baby going by in a stroller squealed and jiggled up and down with him, her blue eyes wide with excitement.

A few of the shopkeepers came out to look. Some seemed pleased to see us. Others looked irritated. And the janitor who was trailing his broom around the storefronts looked positively angry. He mumbled to himself, shooting black looks at us every now and then. What was wrong with him? I wondered.

"Who's for upstairs, who's for downstairs?" asked Nick.

"Sunny can barely walk," Liz said. "She'd better stay up here."

I preferred to get as far away from the Gingerbread House as possible, but I knew she was right.

In the end, Tom, Elmo, and I stayed upstairs and Liz, Nick, and Richelle went downstairs. I watched the backs of three pairs of ears disappearing down the escalator and I turned away to start work.

I really was having trouble walking, and I didn't want to fall flat on my face in front of everyone, so I decided to stay more or less where I was, between the escalator and the pharmacy.

Plenty of people will be coming this way, I told myself. But, of course, I knew that the real reason I'd chosen this spot was that from here I could only see part of the Gingerbread House. The INFORMATION sign blocked my view.

In less than a minute, Mr. Melk, the pharmacist, who was a small man with a mustache, was winking at me as he slid his doors open. Two teenagers and a huge, fat man who'd been waiting outside went into the pastry shop and started looking around. After a while, a skinny man who'd been studying the SPECIALS sign wandered over, took a leaflet from me, and went in, too.

Next door to the pharmacy was the famous opal shop that Mrs. Crumb had talked about. Black opals are extremely rare, and this was the only place in the U.S. with such a huge assortment. It was so fancy that it didn't even have a big shop sign. Just EXCLUSIVE OPALS lettered in gold on its glass door. An elegant-looking sales assistant with dangly opal earrings was moving around inside.

The angry janitor thumped his broom around the front of the opal shop and then moved on to the pharmacy. He frowned at me.

"Get out of the way!" he snarled. He jabbed his broom in my direction, as if I were garbage.

I decided to ignore him. I knew I had a perfect right to be there, and I wasn't doing him or anyone else any harm. Still, it gave me a bad feeling to have him muttering and banging around near me. I wished *he'd* go away. And eventually, he did, pushing past me and grumbling off with his broom. I was glad to see the end of him.

Tom had skipped over to the Gingerbread House with a little girl and her mother. After a moment, I saw him strolling back toward me, handing out leaflets on the way.

"Mrs. C. just put a little blackboard in the window saying there's a special on cream puffs today," he groaned as he passed me. "I'm starving already!"

I handed a leaflet to the fat man as he came out of the pharmacy with a small package. Standing beside me, he seemed even bigger than he had from a distance. He was enormous! His hands were like huge red pieces of steak. His eyes were tiny dark slits surrounded by pouches of fat, and shadowed by thick, bristly black eyebrows.

He glanced at the leaflet, grunted, and immediately wadded it up and dropped it on the ground. *Pig*, I thought. *Why don't you put it in the trash can if you don't want it?*

The fat man lumbered away and began looking in the opal shopwindow. The elegant shop assistant eyed him, unsmiling, from inside.

Another rabbit sidled up to me. For a minute, I didn't know if it was Tom or Elmo. Of course, Tom is much taller, but somehow the identical, smiling, blue-eyed faces confused me.

Then the rabbit spoke to me in Elmo's voice. "See that guy there?" he muttered. "The really big, fat guy, hanging around outside the opal shop?"

I nodded.

"Don't you recognize him?" said Elmo's voice, while the rabbit grinned at me, and its pink ears flapped. "That's The Wolf."

5

The Wolf

I thought he was joking, of course. And I wasn't in the mood for jokes.

"You've got the wrong fairy tale," I said flatly. "There was no wolf in 'Hansel and Gretel.' Only a wicked witch who ate children. Isn't that enough?"

I should have known better. Elmo doesn't usually joke, and he wasn't joking this time.

"Not that wolf," he said impatiently. "The Wolf. You know . . . Sunny, you must have heard of him."

I shook my head. "Is he a wrestler?" I guessed.

Elmo snorted. "No, dummy. He's a criminal."

I slowly turned my head and looked through my wire netting at the man called The Wolf. He'd opened his shopping bag and was gobbling jelly beans from a packet.

"A *criminal*? How do you know?" I whispered.

"*Everyone* knows," said Elmo, ignoring the fact that I obviously didn't. "He runs a huge crime network. Drugs, theft, blackmail, illegal gambling — anything for money."

I didn't doubt him for a minute. Elmo always knows more

than anyone else about people in the news. He loves that sort of thing. And because his father runs the *Pen*, our local newspaper, he gets to know all sorts of inside stuff.

"Why isn't he in jail, then?" I said, staring in fascination at The Wolf.

He threw down the empty jelly bean box and the shopping bag and moved from the opal shop to the men's clothing shop that was next in the row. Just near the door, there was a basket of patterned sweaters with a sign above it saying: PRICES SLASHED.

The Wolf began pulling out the sweaters one by one, looking at sizes. *He'll never find one that fits*, I thought. *He needs Extra Extra Extra Large or something.*

"They can never nail him," said Elmo. "They can never prove anything. He uses other people to do his dirty work for him. And he does it all by some message system. Gives his people their orders and pays them. All without actually meeting them."

"The police should bug his phone," I said.

"They do. And he doesn't do it by phone," Elmo answered. "They don't know *how* he does it. And even if his people get caught, they never talk. Too scared of The Wolf, Dad says. They'd rather go to jail than end up missing."

I could see their point. "What's he doing in Raven Hill?" I whispered.

I saw that the skinny man who had followed The Wolf into the pharmacy had now joined him at the cheap sweaters basket. He had more chance of finding a good fit than The Wolf did.

"He lives here," said Elmo. "And he comes to the mall all the time. I've often seen him. But only in the cold months. He goes to Europe and relaxes for the rest of the year. He hates the heat."

30

"Six months' vacation a year," I said. "Not bad."

"Yeah. He's worth squillions, they say. In Europe, he gambles and parties and skis and all that stuff. But while he's here, he's working," Elmo said. "The cops know that, and they watch him all the time. They check out everything. But they get nowhere. Somehow, he gets his messages through. Right under their noses."

How weird. I shifted uncomfortably.

"What's his real name?" I asked.

"Sidney Wolfe," said Elmo. "But he's always just called The Wolf. He likes it."

The Wolf muttered something to the skinny man, dropped the sweaters he was holding, and walked slowly back out to the plaza. The skinny man stared after him.

"Hey!" I said in excitement. "Look! He said something to that other guy. The other guy's been following The Wolf. And now The Wolf's given him a message. We should tell the police."

Elmo's rabbit face grinned at me as he shook his head. "I'll bet you a hundred bucks that skinny guy *is* a policeman, Sunny. He's been watching The Wolf. But The Wolf's on to him. He was probably just telling him so."

Tom was dancing around in the middle of the plaza, surrounded by a group of little kids. The Wolf stood still and watched him. The thin man left the men's shop and took up his position nearby. He wasn't going to give up.

I went back to handing out leaflets. It was our job, after all. And there were more people coming up the escalators all the time.

The janitor had drifted back to my corner of the plaza by now. He banged his broom and dustpan angrily as he began sweeping up the Gingerbread House leaflets and other trash that had been dropped on the ground since his last round.

"We'd better split up," I said to Elmo in a low voice.

He nodded. Just as he began moving away, I felt a prickling sensation on the back of my neck. Someone was looking at us. I turned around.

The Wolf was staring at me across the plaza, his small black eyes gleaming under his bushy brows. I felt my cheeks begin to burn. I was very glad that my face was hidden by the rabbit head. Glad The Wolf wouldn't know me if he saw me again.

Because the look wasn't friendly. It wasn't friendly at all.

✿

Tom was still hopping around, thrusting leaflets at people, moving closer to the Gingerbread House. He was doing a really good job — unlike me. I decided I'd better be a bit more active, so I shuffled toward the center of the plaza.

From there I could see just about all the shops and watch The Wolf as well. I was interested in him, and I wasn't going to let his black look scare me off.

Of course, now I also had a perfect view of the Gingerbread House. And as usual, my stomach started to churn at the sight of it. I gritted my teeth in irritation. What *was* it about that place that got to me? And for that matter, why was *everything* so strange at the moment?

I like to be sure of things. Unlike Liz, Nick, and Elmo, I don't like questions. And at the moment, my life was full of them.

Who had messed up Burger Joe's shop? And why? Why was

I scared of the Gingerbread House? What had the Work Demons meant when they called out, "You'll be sorry"? How did the man called The Wolf contact his people without seeming to call or talk to anyone? Would my father turn up at gymnastics class this afternoon? Would he like what he saw?

The ground seemed to wobble under my feet. Too many questions. No answers. I frowned under my mask and handed out some more leaflets.

The Wolf went into the bookstore two doors down from the Gingerbread House. His skinny friend followed, and I saw the big man smile.

The Wolf's really enjoying this, I thought suddenly. He was just playing with that detective.

Tom bounced toward the bookstore. I decided that he'd been watching The Wolf, too. Maybe he knew who he was. Or more likely, he just thought he was amazing-looking. Tom likes to draw, and he's always on the lookout for interesting people to sketch.

The Wolf chose a paperback from the table at the front of the bookstore and paid for it at the counter. The skinny policeman, pretending to check out the books himself, watched his every move. The Wolf passed him on the way out, and very deliberately took the book from its bag and flipped through the pages with a huge thumb, right in front of his nose.

He is playing with the policeman, I thought. *He's showing him that there's no message in the book.*

The skinny policeman didn't move, and The Wolf walked on out of the store, laughing. It was an awful laugh. Quite a few shoppers turned to stare.

Tom jumped close to him and held out a leaflet. The Wolf

hesitated, then laughed again and snatched it. He was playing yet another game with the skinny policeman on his trail.

With Tom clowning around beside him, The Wolf lumbered toward the Gingerbread House and looked in the window. Then he pulled open the door and pushed his way inside. His follower wasn't far behind, and it seemed to me that he looked very sharply at Tom as he passed him.

6

Warning signs

Tom was going to get himself into trouble if he wasn't careful. I walked toward him as fast as I could. He was peering through the shopwindow.

"Tom!" I muttered as soon as I got close enough. "Tom, keep away from that big guy. He's dangerous. He's The Wolf."

"Sunny, is that rabbit head pressing too hard on your brain or something?" Tom's muffled voice laughed. "A big bad wolf? In Raven Hill Mall?"

"Tom, this is serious," I snapped, keeping an eye on the Gingerbread House door.

"It certainly is," he said, pressing his nose against the window glass. "That big jerk is buying the last two cream puffs. I'd marked them for my morning snack."

"*Tom!*" I exclaimed, pulling at his arm. "*Get away!*"

Eventually, he did as he was told and went dancing off to tease a group of women standing outside the opal shop. The elegant shop assistant wouldn't be too pleased about that, I thought, but at least Tom was out of harm's way.

The Wolf came back out into the plaza dragging one of Mrs. Crumb's huge, fluffy cream puffs from its paper bag. He bit into it hungrily. Vanilla custard squeezed out over his fingers. He sucked at them before stuffing the rest of the pastry into his mouth and walking off, chewing.

The skinny policeman looked at me as he, too, left the Gingerbread House. Then he gazed across the plaza at Tom. I saw his eyes narrow slightly. Then he turned away and strode off after The Wolf, who was heading for the escalator.

Well, that's the end of that bit of excitement, I thought, as first The Wolf and then his follower stepped onto the escalator and disappeared from view.

But, of course, it was only the beginning.

❂

At eleven o'clock exactly, we all crowded down the Staff Only corridor that ran behind the Gingerbread House and all the other shops on that side of the plaza.

We piled through the kitchen door and thankfully pulled off our heads.

"Wow, your faces are red!" chortled the cheerful Julie, wiping sweat from her gleaming forehead with the back of her hand.

"We've been stuck inside these things," said Nick, waving his rabbit head at her. "What's your excuse?"

Julie's grin broadened. She wasn't in the least offended. "I'm always red," she said. "My mom's the same way. And the ovens don't help." She pulled open one of the big black doors in the wall in front of her. A wave of heat billowed out.

"They wouldn't," said Liz, gazing at the dark, gaping hole. "Geez, that one's big enough to hold a person!"

"Too true," agreed Julie, bending forward to pull trays of golden, delicious-smelling pastries from deep inside the oven. "Wouldn't want someone to push you from behind while you were doing this, would you? You'd be a baked bunny in no time."

She laughed uproariously. Nick and Richelle exchanged glances. They obviously didn't think too much of Julie.

"Do we get to eat now?" asked Tom. The kitchen smells were getting to him.

"Oh, sure," Julie said. She picked up two trays of pastries and pushed through the swinging door to the shop. Through the opening I could see a crowd of people waiting at the counter. And one of them looked familiar.

"Hey!" I exclaimed as the door swung shut. "Nutley Frean's out there."

"Yeah?" In two seconds Nick was at the door, pushing it open a crack. He peered out. "He is, too," he reported.

"What's he doing?" demanded Liz.

"Just hanging around with his hands in his pockets," muttered Nick, his eye glued to the crack in the door.

"Can you see Julie?" asked Tom hungrily. "What's she getting for us?"

"Tom," sighed Richelle. "You're just a *pig*."

I found a glass in a cupboard, went to the sink, and helped myself to some water. Surely, I didn't need Mrs. Crumb's permission to do that.

"Stand back," said Nick, moving away from the door. "Big Julie's on her way."

The door burst open, and Julie appeared with a tray scattered with assorted cakes and pastries in her hands, and three empty trays under her arm.

"The old girl's thrilled to death with you," she announced. "Stuff's going like hotcakes out there! Haw, haw, haw!"

"Are these for us?" asked Tom, eyeing the tray.

"Sure thing," Julie grinned. "Dig in." She helped herself to a large meringue and began munching happily. Everyone crowded around. Even Richelle. And, I have to admit, even me. There were some candied fruits there that really looked good.

"Cream puffs!" exclaimed Tom, pouncing on the biggest. "I thought they were all gone."

"Nope. She was serving most people from under the counter once the first tray was nearly gone," mumbled Julie with her mouth full. "She often does that with the specials. Likes people to think the stuff's running out fast, I guess. She's a smart one, Mrs. Crumb."

"Have you been here long?" asked Liz absentmindedly, her fingers hovering between a chocolate éclair and a strawberry tart.

"Ever since the shop opened," said Julie proudly. "I help with the cooking, do the deliveries, and clean the shop after hours. Mrs. C. and I get along great." She took another bite of meringue.

There was a crash as the swing door burst open.

"Julie!" thundered a voice.

We all spun around guiltily, as though we'd been caught stealing food.

Mrs. Crumb was standing there with her back against the

38

door, a tray in her hands. Her chest was heaving, her eyes flashing with fury.

Julie's cheeks flushed an even deeper red. "Um . . . yes, Mrs. Crumb?" she spluttered, trying to swallow the meringue in her mouth.

Mrs. Crumb held out the tray of golden pastries. "WHAT . . . IS . . . THIS?" she thundered.

We all blinked at her. And then Julie gasped, Tom made a choking sound, and Richelle screamed.

Lying on one corner of the tray was a very stiff, very dead mouse.

7

Disgusting!

Julie's hand flew to her mouth. "H-h-how did that get there?" she spluttered, her eyes goggling.

"Is it . . . cooked?" asked Elmo curiously.

Richelle screamed again.

Nick quietly put down his half-eaten chocolate éclair. "Charming," he said.

Mrs. Crumb swept to the garbage container by the back door and tipped the contents of the tray into it.

"Luckily, very luckily, I saw the thing in the window before anyone else did." She gritted her teeth. "Julie, do you have any *idea* what would have happened if I hadn't?"

Julie gulped. She twisted her apron between her big hands.

"Mrs. Crumb, honestly, that mouse wasn't there when I took the pastries out to you," she said. "It wasn't. I would have seen it. It must have climbed onto the tray out in the shop, and died there. It must —"

Mrs. Crumb threw the empty tray onto the bench with a clatter.

"Julie, be *quiet!*" she barked. "There's no possible excuse for this. That creature has been dead for days. It probably died in the oven and fell onto the tray when you put the pastries in. Disgusting!" She shuddered.

"Mrs. Crumb —" the girl began.

But Mrs. Crumb waved her away.

"I've left a shop full of people out there," she snapped. "I'll deal with you later."

She strode to the swing door and went back out to the shop.

Julie looked helplessly after her for a moment. Then she spun around to face us, her eyes suddenly alight with hope. "You kids saw me take the trays out," she exclaimed. "You didn't see that mouse, did you?"

We all shook our heads.

"But I couldn't swear it *wasn't* there, either," said Nick. "Could you, Liz?"

Liz wrinkled her nose. I could see that she would have loved to help Julie out. But she couldn't.

"I didn't look closely enough," she said sadly.

"Me, neither," added Elmo.

Richelle just shivered quietly.

"Well, I did," Tom broke in. "I looked *very* closely at those trays. And there wasn't any mouse."

Julie clasped her hands and drew a relieved breath. "Oh," she whispered. "Then you can tell Mrs. Crumb!"

Tom nodded. "I'll tell her," he said. "Don't worry, Julie."

Nick snorted.

"Tom, are you sure about this?" I asked suspiciously. Unlike Liz, Tom was quite capable of bending the truth to get someone out of trouble.

"Of course I am," he said. "Would I lie?"

"Yes!" Nick, Liz, Elmo, and Richelle answered together. Everyone started arguing loudly.

Julie looked as if she was going to start crying. I didn't think I could stand that. And also, the more I thought about it, the more I thought she was being blamed unfairly.

It seemed quite possible to me that someone like Julie could serve up a dead mouse on a tray of pastries without noticing it was there. Like some of the people in my gymnastics class, she had a lot more energy than brains. You could tell by the way she banged and rushed around the kitchen.

But she plainly worked like a dog to keep this place gleaming. It was spotless. I couldn't believe there'd be a long-dead mouse in the oven.

And, then, there was something else. A niggling suspicion. Something I couldn't prove, but . . .

"Listen," I said. The others went on arguing, so I took a breath and tried again.

"*Listen!*" I repeated loudly. "Stop it, and listen."

Finally, they quieted down and looked at me. "What if the mouse wasn't on the tray when it went out to the shop . . . ?" I said slowly and clearly. "Just say it wasn't, for now. Then how did it get there?"

"I put the trays down on the side of the counter while I cleared space for them in the window," mumbled Julie. "The mouse must have crawled on then and died, and —"

"No, that won't work," snapped Nick. "Like Mrs. Crumb said, that mouse has been dead a lot longer than five minutes. If it got on the tray after you left the kitchen, it must have fallen onto it. From one of those shelves behind the counter, or something." He shrugged his shoulders. "I suppose it could have happened like that."

"Seems unlikely," said Elmo. "Without anyone seeing it fall, anyway. The shop was crowded."

I decided it was time to tell them my theory.

"What if it was put there deliberately?" I said. "By someone standing near the counter."

"But-but who would do that, Sunny?" stammered Liz. "Who on earth would . . . ?" Then her face changed.

"Nutley Frean," breathed Nick. *"Nutley Frean!* He was there. Sunny saw him. I saw him."

"Yes!" Tom banged his fist into his palm. "With his hands in his pockets. Waiting for his chance to . . ."

Julie was looking bewildered. "Who are you talking about?" she asked.

"This guy we know," said Liz slowly. "A member of the gang who wanted to work here instead of us."

"They called out, 'You'll be sorry!' when they left," I reminded them. "And if any of the customers had seen that mouse, Mrs. Crumb *would* have been sorry, wouldn't she?"

"The whole mall would have heard about it in ten minutes," said Elmo. "And she'd have had a visit from the health inspectors, for sure."

"How *embarrassing*," said Richelle. "It would have been just like Burger Joe's!"

We looked at one another.

"Yes," Liz said grimly. "Just like Burger Joe's."

○

We talked for a bit longer, and then Mrs. Crumb poked her head back into the kitchen, put a huge bundle of leaflets on the bench beside the door, and frowned at us. It was time to go back to work.

"We'll tell her about Nutley Frean when we finish," Liz said as we trooped out, watched by a downcast Julie. "And I suppose we should tell Joe, too. It's obvious now who messed up his kitchen. Those . . . those *rats* did it. Because he hired us instead of them. Can you *believe* it?"

"I can," said Nick. "But no one else will. We've got no proof."

"But we've got to *do* something!" Liz raged. "We can't just let them get away with it."

"No," agreed Richelle, brushing down her fur. "Because, I mean, they'll just go on doing it, won't they? To anyone who chooses us instead of them."

We all looked at her. From out of that murky soup Richelle calls a brain had popped the really important point . . . as so often happens.

The Work Demons were out to get us. And they didn't care who else they hurt to do it. If we didn't stop them, Help-for-Hire Inc. would be finished.

We'd reached the plaza by now, and people were staring and

smiling at us. "We'll talk about it after work," said Liz firmly. "Then we'll see."

We were to finish at two-thirty, but I knew I wouldn't be able to hang around with them and talk anything over. I had that gymnastics class at three. The class my father was supposed to come and watch. I'd put it out of my mind, but as I walked across to my place near the pharmacy, I started to think about it again.

Like I said, I don't get scared. But I do get nervous. Sometimes. And this was one of those times. My dad coaches champions. He's too old to play the big tennis tournaments himself now, of course. But the kids he coaches do. They're really high-powered. And he's got very high standards.

I didn't want him deciding I was no good, or my coach wasn't, or anything like that. I wanted him to know that we had high standards, too. And that you didn't have to go and live in a faraway place like Australia to be a champion.

No matter what he thought.

8

A big decision

I was still jittery when I got to the gym, but once I'd changed and started warming up, all the nerves began slipping away. The gym is like my second home, I guess. Everything about it is so familiar: the equipment, the sounds, the lights — even the smell of it.

Once or twice, I glanced over to where visitors usually stood to watch, but my father wasn't there. *He probably won't come after all*, I thought. I didn't know if I was glad or sorry.

Hong, my coach, got our small class together and started putting us through our paces.

At first, I knew I was relaxing. Then I forgot everything but what I was doing. It always happens like that. At the gym, it's as though I slip into a sort of private space, where nothing can get at me. It's as though everything from outside just ceases to exist.

I guess a lot of people have a way into a private space. With my sister Cathy, it's the piano. When she's playing, nothing else matters. You can see it in her face.

Liz says writing stories does the same thing for her. And sometimes working on craft projects. She really loves all that sort of thing. Tom says painting does it for him. With Nick, it's computer and video games. With Elmo, it's reading. I don't know about Richelle. Maybe for her it's shopping.

Anyway, for that hour in the gym, I escaped from time and space, from Burger Joe's and the Gingerbread House, from The Wolf, and from the Work Demons and Dad and everything else.

At the end, I felt great. It had been a good class. I knew I'd done well. Hong gave me one of those short little nods that meant he was pleased.

And only then did I remember my father. I turned to look and there he was, outside in the observation area, smiling at me through the glass. Black hair, red sweater, white shirt, white teeth. I lifted my hand to wave to him.

"That's Roy Chan!" I heard someone say.

"He's Sunny's dad," someone else whispered. "Didn't you know?"

A hand touched my shoulder. "I didn't know *Roy Chan* was your *father*, Sunny," this girl named Madeline said excitedly. "How fantastic! Do you think I could get his autograph?"

I shrugged. "I guess so," I said.

I started walking to the door. For some reason, I was shivering all over. I had the feeling that something was about to happen. Something important.

✿

"So what do you think, Sunny?" Mom asked me calmly when I got home. "Do you want to go to Australia to live with Roy for a while?"

47

I didn't say anything. I just sat on the edge of my bed and looked at her.

I didn't know what I wanted.

I thought back an hour. I was sitting in the Black Cat Café with my father. He was leaning across the table, his eyes sparkling.

"You'll love Sydney," he was saying to me. "And you'll get the best training there. The best."

"What about school?" I asked. It was a stupid question, because I knew I could go to school in Sydney. But I was just so shocked.

And I guess "What about school?" stood for lots of other questions — like, "What about my friends?" "What about Mom, and the things I do every day?" "What about my life? The only life I know."

But Dad wasn't about to understand that. He waved his hand and laughed. "Don't worry about a thing," he said. "Trust me. The important thing is, we'll be together. And I can help you. You've got what it takes. I saw that earlier today. There were a few ragged edges, but the talent's there. The talent, and the drive. And with me behind you, the sky's the limit."

I just sat there drinking my apple juice. My mind was racing.

He laughed again. "Take it all very calmly, don't you?" he said. "That's my girl."

I jerked back to the present. Mom was speaking to me again. "You're probably feeling a bit confused and scared, as well as excited, Sunny," she was saying. "It's a big thing for you. You need time to think about it. Take what you need."

"Dad just takes it for granted I'm going," I murmured. "He expects me to leave with him on Saturday. He's going to book my ticket tonight."

"I know," Mom said ruefully. "He's like that. But it's still your decision, Sunny. And today's only Monday. You've got your passport. If you decide to go, you can pack a bag in an hour. Everything else could be sent later. Or, if you decide not to go, the plane ticket can be canceled. See? There's no hurry."

"Mom, what do you think?" I asked. But I knew it was a pointless question.

She looked at me steadily. "It's not up to me," she said, as I'd been sure she would. "It's up to you. Whatever you decide, I'm with you all the way."

I watched her face, but it didn't change. For a moment, I was almost angry with her. For a moment, I wanted her to behave like, say, Nick's mother would have if he'd been thinking about moving far away: She could cry, cling, beg me not to go, not to leave her.

But that wasn't Mom's way. It never had been and never would.

She got up and started wandering around the bedroom, touching things.

"I always knew that one day your father would come back for you," she murmured, almost as if she were talking to herself. "You were always his favorite. The only one of the children he ever spent much time with. He'd read to you every night he was home. He took you everywhere. Played games with you. You know, I've told you."

I nodded.

She sighed. "It's interesting. It's as if he knew, even when you were only a little thing, that you'd be what you are. So good at sports, I mean. So good at anything physical. The only one of the five who inherited his gifts. I guess that's where the bond between you two comes from."

"He hardly ever came to see me," I said.

"No." My mother's slim, strong doctor's hands — the hands that bandaged injuries, massaged tight muscles, and comforted people who were sick or in pain — lightly brushed the top of my desk chair. "He's like that. Always busy. Things to do, places to go, people to see," she sighed. "And tennis to play, of course. Always tennis to play."

She turned around to face me. She smiled. "I guess he thought you'd still be here later. And he couldn't have looked after a little girl. He's not organized enough for that. It's different now. You can practically look after yourself. You're all grown up."

Was I? I stared into the mirror on the closet opposite my bed. My reflection stared back at me. Shiny black hair tied back in a ponytail, dark almond eyes, blue tracksuit. Sunny Chan, all grown up. Ready to face the world.

"The sky's the limit," Dad had said.

"Think about it," Mom had said. "Whatever you decide, I'm with you all the way."

I took a deep breath. My stomach churned with a mixture of excitement and nervousness. Australia, star coaching, travel with my famous, charismatic father? Or home, safety, the familiar routine with my calm, hardworking mother?

Which was I going to choose? At the end of this week, would I be in Raven Hill, or flying to the other side of the world?

Only I could answer that question. And I didn't have the faintest idea.

9

Bad dreams

Liz called, just as we were finishing dinner, to say that the gang had decided to talk to Mrs. Crumb about the Work Demons first thing in the morning. She asked me to show up early and meet at the INFORMATION sign like before.

At first, I found it quite hard to concentrate on what she was saying. Since Dad's talk with me, my mind had been so full of him and Sydney and everything that I hadn't given the Gingerbread House or the Work Demons a thought. It all seemed very far away, somehow.

But for Liz, of course, it was the most important thing there was. She talked on and on about it. It was weird to sit there in the kitchen with Mom, Penny, Cathy, Amy, and Sarah looking on, listening to Liz and feeling so cut off.

I could have told Liz what was on my mind. After all, she was my best friend. If she'd found out she might be leaving Raven Hill, she'd have called me first thing. To talk about it, get rid of some of her mixed-up feelings.

I could have done that. "I might be going to Sydney,

52

Australia, to live," I could have said. "I might be going at the end of the week. With my father."

But what if I had?

"Sunny!" she'd have screamed. "Oh, Sunny, *no!*"

And whatever she said afterward, that first reaction would have been the truth. Liz wouldn't want me to go. I knew that. Maybe that's why I didn't tell her. Like Mom said, I had to think this through by myself.

"Sunny, are you OK?" Liz asked suddenly.

I suppose I'd sounded a little out of it.

"Sure, I'm OK," I said as normally as I could. "I'm just tired."

I saw Cathy raise her eyebrows at Mom, who shook her head slightly. Penny poured herself more coffee. Amy and Sarah looked at each other and then went back to their dessert.

My sisters all knew by now that Dad had asked me to go home with him. But they hadn't talked to me about it. They were leaving me alone, as Mom had no doubt asked them to do. And anyway, they probably weren't all that interested, I realized. They're much older than me, and it wouldn't make much difference to them if I left.

Except for Cathy, I thought, as I said good-bye to Liz, hung up, mumbled something to the others, and made my way upstairs. With me gone, she'd get a bedroom to herself. She'd probably like that.

For some reason, all the excitement had gone out of me now, and I felt flat and tired. In fact, I felt exhausted. I pulled off my clothes, crawled into bed, and almost immediately went to sleep.

But all night, I dreamed. Long, complicated, worrying dreams. About Dad, and Mom, my sisters, the gym, school, Hong, the Help-for-Hire gang. And wherever my dream was set, one thing kept appearing over and over again.

The Gingerbread House.

✿

The main entrance was locked when I got to the mall the next morning. How was I supposed to meet the others on the first floor? I looked at my watch. I was a little bit early, maybe.

I hung around for a while and then saw the woman from the opal shop arrive in a taxi and go into another door tucked away at the side. A staff entrance. Of course! Liz had probably told me about it last night. I really hadn't been listening to her properly.

"You're an early bird, Suzanne," a security guard sitting at a desk was saying to the woman as I pushed the door open. He was a chiseled, dapper sort of man with blue eyes and an Irish accent.

The opal shop woman nodded briefly to him and went through another door that seemed to lead into the ground floor of the mall.

The security guard grinned and rubbed his square chin. "Nervous as a cat," he said to me. "Don't blame her. She's got a crowd coming in today, and all those opals to look after. Worth a mint, they are. Now, what can I do for you? Mall isn't open yet."

"Can I go up to the first floor?" I asked him. "I'm one of Mrs. Crumb's rabbits."

He grinned. "I'd have known you anywhere," he teased. "Sure, go on up and join the party then. And good luck to you."

"Are the others inside already?" I asked, glancing at my watch again.

"Well, Hazel Crumb and Julie are, of course. But there's just the one of you kids so far," said the security guard. "Sent him up a while ago. Black-haired fella."

Nick, I thought.

I thanked the guard and went through the door to the mall. It was dim and deserted. The only movement seemed to be the silver escalators running smoothly, endlessly, up and down between the floors.

I stepped onto the escalator and glided up through the shadows. Cooking smells filled the first floor, but the steel shutters were still locked over the Gingerbread House windows.

There was no one waiting by the INFORMATION sign.

Nick must have gone around the back already, I thought. He can never bear to wait.

Well, I wasn't going to wait, either, staring at the Gingerbread House with only the purring of the escalators for company. For some reason, the place didn't give me such a bad feeling all closed and shuttered, but memories of my dreams were still hanging around like a dull headache.

Besides, Suzanne, or whatever her name was, was staring at me from the opal shop window, as if she thought I was up to no good. I had enough problems without coping with her.

With my head bent to avoid looking at the Gingerbread House, I walked over to the short hallway that led to the restrooms. My feet made small squeaky sounds on the tiled floor of the plaza. The escalators continued purring. I could feel Suzanne's eyes burning into the back of my neck.

Just as I turned into the hallway there was a scuffle, a thump, and a swishing sound. My head jerked up, but there was nothing to be seen. The hallway was empty. But the door to the men's room was still swinging a bit. Someone had just ducked in there. Fast.

Nick? But if so, why the rush? Was he trying to play some trick on me? Planning to jump out and scare me? Surely not. That wasn't Nick's style. Tom's maybe, but not Nick's. Well, then, it was just a coincidence that the scuffle happened as I turned into the hallway. Nick, or someone else, needed to go to the restroom in a hurry. So what? No law against that, was there?

Ignoring the prickling in my spine, I walked past the men's room door to the end of the hallway and looked down the Staff Only passage that branched off from it. Light streamed from the Gingerbread House kitchen door. I could even hear Mrs. Crumb's voice. She was speaking very loudly.

No sign of Nick. No sound of Nick's voice. So it must have been him in the restroom after all.

I decided to go back to the INFORMATION sign and wait. It was stupid, prowling around like this on my own. It was because I was all stirred up. I had to pull myself together. Put Dad, and Australia, and my big decision out of my mind for a while.

I walked back to the plaza, and there by the INFORMATION sign were Liz, Elmo, and Richelle. Liz was checking her watch. I jogged over to them.

"Mrs. Crumb's in the kitchen," I said. "Nick'll be here in a sec. Where's Tom?"

"Probably eating somewhere," Liz said, and sighed. "Honestly, it's impossible trying to organize you people sometimes."

Richelle opened her mouth to protest, but then her eyes widened. She was looking over my shoulder.

Liz and I turned around and saw Julie rushing across the plaza toward the escalator. She was wearing a jacket and clutching a handbag. Her face was burning red, and tears were pouring down her cheeks. She saw us and hesitated, pressing both hands over her mouth.

Liz and I ran over to her. "Julie, what's wrong?" Liz gasped. "What's happened?"

"I-I've been fired!" choked Julie. "Mrs. Crumb — she told me to get out. She was so *furious*. Oh —" She buried her face in her hands.

Liz put her arm around the girl's plump, heaving shoulders.

"But what happened?" I asked. "Why did she fire you?"

"First, she found some big, dead cockroaches lying behind the garbage bin in the kitchen," wailed Julie. "And she yelled at me for that. But then — just now — oh, I can't believe it!"

"What?" I urged. I couldn't stand this.

"It was the raisin-bran muffins," Julie sobbed. "Oh, they'd have been lovely ones, too. You can always tell. Nice plump raisins. And the batter was so light, and —"

"Julie, what *happened*?" urged Liz. Out of the corner of my eye, I saw Tom and Nick moving toward us. Richelle, of course, was keeping well out of the way.

"I was filling the muffin pans," Julie wept. "And Mrs. Crumb came in from the shop. And she looked in the mixing bowl and — and —"

"What?" demanded Nick, frowning impatiently.

"And the batter was — was full of flies," cried Julie. "Big, fat, dead flies!"

10

In the kitchen

Even Tom shuddered.

We were all thinking the same thing. If the batter had made it into the oven and the muffins had been cooked, the flies would have looked a lot like the raisins.

"People could have eaten them — *we* could have eaten them — without realizing," Nick muttered, looking sick.

"At first," Tom said. "And then there'd be a strange taste, or something . . . crunchy . . . in your mouth. And then you'd have looked. And then . . . there'd have been some legs, or a wing, or half a body, and you'd know . . ."

"Oh, Tom, be quiet!" exclaimed Liz. "It's disgusting."

"That's what Mrs. Crumb said," sobbed Julie. "Disgusting. She said I must have left the batter uncovered and the screen door open so the flies got in. I admit I did leave the kitchen for a minute. Just to go into the storeroom, because I'd forgotten the pans. But honestly, I was away only for two seconds."

"The fatal two seconds," Tom said under his breath.

"Mrs. Crumb said I was a menace," whispered Julie. "First, the mouse, now this. She said to get out, and never come back!"

You could understand that, I thought.

"Are you going to tell her about that boy yesterday, and the mouse?" Julie asked Liz, her lips trembling. "You said you'd tell her."

"Sure, Julie," Liz said quickly. "We'll tell her we saw Nutley in the shop. But you know she might not believe he put the mouse on the tray." She paused. "Especially now," she added, as gently as she could.

Julie wiped her eyes with the back of her hand. "Well, try your best, will you?" she pleaded. "I can't afford to lose my job. I really can't. Oh —" Her eyes filled with tears again. "Oh, what's my mom going to say?"

I saw Nick nudge Liz in the ribs. He wanted to end this conversation. Liz patted Julie's shoulder awkwardly. "Well, we'd better get going now, Julie," she said. "We'll see you."

"Yeah," Julie sniffled. "Yeah. See you."

We all moved off toward the Gingerbread House. I looked back once and saw Julie still standing there, looking after us.

"Poor thing," Liz whispered to me.

"Silly thing, you mean," I couldn't help saying. "Look, yeah, I'm sorry for her, but how would you like a mouthful of flies for breakfast? She should have been more careful."

"Looks like that mouse thing probably wasn't Nutley after all," Nick pointed out. "We've gotten here early for nothing."

"What a bore," yawned Richelle.

"We'll still have to tell Mrs. Crumb about that," said Liz. "I promised Julie."

Richelle sighed. "What does that matter?" she said. "Julie's been fired because of something quite different and just as disgusting. And she did it all on her own. No one else was there."

"Except the cockroaches. And the flies," Tom put in.

Everyone groaned.

We went around to the back door of the Gingerbread House. Mrs. Crumb was rushing around in the kitchen, looking more hassled than we'd ever seen her.

But when she saw us, her eyes lit up. She smiled and beckoned, and my stomach turned over. Not as badly as the first few times, though. *Maybe I'm finally getting over this childish thing, whatever it is*, I thought.

"What a blessing!" Mrs. Crumb was saying. "I'm —" She hesitated. Of course, she didn't know we'd seen Julie. "I'm on my own today," she went on, deciding to keep it simple. "Since you're here so early, could you give me a hand? I'll pay extra, of course."

"Sure," said Nick. "No problem."

She beamed at him, her nose nearly touching her chin. My spine crawled.

Then she started rushing again, barking orders, clattering pans and trays. It obviously wasn't the time for Liz to start chattering about dead mice or Work Demons. Luckily, Liz could see this as well as I could, and she didn't even try.

Within minutes, Nick and Liz were ferrying cakes and muffins into the front of the shop, Tom was washing up, I was wiping and packing things away, Elmo was cleaning the benches, and Richelle was perched gracefully on a high stool, nibbling a cookie and listening to Mrs. Crumb.

"How does she *do* it?" Tom hissed, clattering the dishes and glaring at Richelle. "We're slaving away as usual and she's —"

I shushed him. I wanted to hear what Mrs. Crumb was talking about.

"Now, Richelle," she was saying, rapidly squeezing dabs of cream onto tiny meringues, "do you think you can manage in the shop on your own?"

"Oh, sure," Richelle said carelessly, kicking her leg and watching her toe as it pointed and flexed.

"I can't really afford to put one of the others with you," frowned Mrs. Crumb. "I need as many rabbits outside as possible. Do you see?"

"Oh, sure," Richelle said again. "That's cool. I'm better on my own, anyway. The others would just get in my way."

Mrs. Crumb beamed at her.

If you go to Australia, a voice in my head whispered, *you won't have to put up with Richelle anymore.*

I went to the storeroom to put some things away, and then stood at the door for a moment, looking back into the busy kitchen. Tom was singing some silly song over the dishes in the sink. Elmo was attacking the benches in the determined way he does everything. Liz and Nick were moving through the swinging door carrying tray after tray, plate after plate, of delicious-looking cakes. Richelle was checking out her fingernails, half-listening as Mrs. Crumb talked on.

None of them knew what was happening to me.

It was very strange. Lately, everything was so strange.

✿

Tom heaved the last of the pans onto the drain board with a sigh of relief.

"At last," he said. "Now I need food. Any flies around? No, not a one. Oh, dear. Have to make do with a cookie, won't I?"

He helped himself to one.

"You must have a tapeworm, Moysten," jeered Nick, noticing. "You had double pancakes and hash browns this morning."

"So did you," Tom pointed out.

"Yeah," said Nick. "But I hadn't had breakfast before that, like you. And I'm not hungry again now, am I?"

"Stop arguing," I started to say. And then I ran the conversation back in my mind. Something was odd here.

"Wait a minute," I said, turning to Nick. "How do you know what Tom ate? How does he know what you ate?"

He stared at me. "Because we met at the diner," he said finally. "How do you think?"

"But you were here in the mall long before Tom was," I said. Now they were all staring at me.

"No, he wasn't," Tom said finally. "We arrived together."

"But —"

I broke off and remembered what the security guard had said. He said he'd sent a "black-haired fella" up to the Gingerbread House. He'd assumed the person was one of Mrs. Crumb's rabbits, because that's who the person said he was. *I* had assumed it was Nick.

But Nick still must have been at the diner with Tom when I arrived at the mall. Someone else with black hair was up here at the Gingerbread House — or at least lurking around outside it. And suddenly, I knew who that was.

"What's up with you, Sunny?" demanded Tom. "Come on, spit it out."

"I know how the flies got into the muffins," I said, and looked around for Mrs. Crumb.

11

All sorts of trouble

"I can't believe this!" Mrs. Crumb was furious. "You mean those boys have been planting things to make this shop look like a health risk?"

I nodded. "I'm sure of it," I said firmly. "Darren Henshaw was around here this morning. With a pocket full of dead flies and cockroaches, I'll bet."

"And we think the same thing happened at Burger Joe's," Liz added.

Mrs. Crumb's frown deepened. "How *dare* they!" she hissed.

"It's because you hired us instead of them," said Liz. "We're sorry."

"Sorry!" thundered Mrs. Crumb, suddenly losing her cool completely. "*Sorry?* Do you realize I could have ended up with health inspectors crawling all over this place? Do you know how disastrous that would have been for me?"

Liz shrank back. "Do-do you want us to go?" she stammered.

Mrs. Crumb stopped raging and pressed her lips together. She was breathing hard, fighting for control.

"No, of course not," she said slowly, at last. "Why should you go?"

She looked around at our startled expressions, and a grim smile spread over her face.

"I'm sorry I shouted," she said. "I lose my temper too easily. But I'm not angry with you. I'm angry with them. And I'm going to give them a lesson they'll never forget."

"What are you going to do?" asked Nick curiously.

Mrs. Crumb rubbed her long chin. "Nothing yet," she muttered. "Just now, I haven't got time. But they'll be sorry they tangled with me. Very sorry."

I saw Nick put on his superior look behind her back. He didn't think anything Mrs. Crumb could do would worry the Work Demons.

But watching her tight lips and cold eyes as she turned back to her work, I wasn't so sure.

✿

By eight-thirty we were in our rabbit suits and out prowling the mall with our leaflets. My suit felt no more comfortable this morning than it had yesterday, and I decided to stay put on the first floor again.

I felt a bit envious as I watched the others scurry around, hopping up and down the escalators. They'd decided to move around more today in order to keep an eye out for Work Demons. I soon lost track of who was who.

Mrs. Crumb hadn't been able to get Julie on the phone to

ask her to come back. So Richelle was behind the counter of the Gingerbread House on her own.

We were all a bit nervous about this, but as Nick said, it was Mrs. Crumb's decision and at least we knew Richelle would get the money right. Richelle is clueless about most things, but her mind's like a steel trap when it comes to money.

Anyway, there I was back in my old spot by the escalator. Mr. Melk, the pharmacist, waved to me. Suzanne in Exclusive Opals came to her door, saw me, raised her penciled eyebrows, and turned up her nose. The crabby janitor came bumping around, scowling. Everything was as it had been the day before.

I handed out leaflets, feeling rather bored. I almost wished The Wolf would come shopping again, to give me something to look at.

Time passed slowly. A small woman with glasses went into the opal shop. The owner of the men's shop started decorating his window with T-shirts reading: WELCOME TO SUNNY RAVEN HILL. Getting ready for the tourists, no doubt.

Dad's right, I thought suddenly. *Why stay stuck here, in Raven Hill, going to school and doing dead-end, boring jobs for peanuts when I could be moving on?*

I thought about it. No one but Liz, and maybe my mother, would miss me. And Liz had the rest of the gang, and Mom had her work and my sisters. The place I filled in their world wouldn't stay empty for long.

I shuffled my feet on the slippery tiles of the plaza. I felt unsettled and uncomfortable. It wasn't just the rabbit suit or the job. This place was getting me down. I wasn't myself. I knew it.

For a start, why on earth was I still so affected by Hazel Crumb and the Gingerbread House? Mrs. Crumb only had to smile and beckon to make me break out in a sweat. And the sight of the Gingerbread House still made me feel sick and scared. That showed how nervous I'd gotten. I needed to get away from all of it.

I saved my tail from being pulled by a small boy in a super-hero suit and gave a leaflet to his father. *I've made my decision*, I thought. *I'll go with Dad. It's a chance I can't pass up. It came at just the right time for me.*

I caught sight of a rabbit dancing around by the INFOR-MATION sign, surrounded by a group of kids. *Tom acting up again*, I thought. Well, at least he was having a good time. I watched as he pretended to fall over. The kids screamed with laughter.

There was a chattering sound from the escalator. I looked around and saw that it was suddenly loaded. A mass of inter-ested faces stared up at me as they rose slowly to the first floor. The tourist buses had arrived.

I began handing out leaflets to the tourists as they passed me on their way to Exclusive Opals. I couldn't reach them all, but I could see that the others were closing in, making sure no one was missed.

Tom bounced into the crowd with the kids trailing him. Another one of us was moving in from one side. I could see two pairs of ears at the bottom of the escalator, coming up. And big blue eyes and pink ears right in the thick of things, near the opal shop.

The tourists seemed to like it. They were taking photographs, talking and smiling. I nodded and smiled back at them as I handed out my leaflets.

Out of the corner of my eye I could see the janitor fussing around the garbage can, in the center of the crowd. Maybe he was hoping that some of the foreigners would think it was an American custom to give tips to janitors.

A steady stream of people had begun disappearing into Exclusive Opals. Soon the shop would be packed, and the escalator was still crowded.

Mr. Melk came outside to look. So did someone from the men's shop. And I saw that in the bookstore across the plaza a huge display of glossy books marked "Americana" had taken the place of the paperback novels that The Wolf had looked through the day before.

It seemed as though everyone wanted to make the most of the tourist invasion. The tourists might have come for Raven Hill's famous opals — but why shouldn't they buy T-shirts, suntan lotion, and guidebooks as well?

I noticed that the small woman with glasses was pushing back through the crowd toward me. No wonder she'd left Exclusive Opals. As she reached me, I handed her a leaflet.

I think it was around then that the alarm began to ring.

Fire! I thought, my heart leaping.

But it wasn't fire, as I soon discovered.

"Stop, thief!" shrilled a voice. "Stop that woman! There! With the rabbit! Stop her!"

And in seconds, we were surrounded.

✿

Suzanne was hysterical. Her glossy brown hair was falling down from its neat roll in hard, sprayed wisps. Her lipstick was smudged. It was as though her smooth surface had cracked.

No wonder she was upset. Black opals are rare. And the ring she said the woman with me had stolen was worth a small fortune.

"She definitely took it!" she was calling out. "Definitely! She had it on, and when the tourist group came in, I turned away for a minute, and then she was gone in the crowd. She was wearing the ring, I tell you!"

A circle of interested faces pressed in around us. I stood there in my ridiculous rabbit suit, feeling like an intruder.

The small woman pushed her glasses back on her nose and stood her ground.

"I certainly don't have that ring," she said angrily. "I put it back down on the counter before I left the shop. Look!"

She spread out her hands. Her fingers were bare.

Suzanne gritted her teeth. "She's got it on her somewhere," she screeched. "She's hidden it. Search her."

"Would you mind coming with me, ma'am?" rumbled a calm voice I recognized. It was the Irish-American security guard from downstairs. "It might be best if we discussed this in private," he added.

"Yes, it might," agreed the small woman calmly. She turned to Suzanne. "I'll be happy to be searched," she went on. "Very

70

happy. And then I'll be calling my lawyer. How dare you accuse me of theft!"

It was quite obvious from her voice that she meant every word she said. I thought Suzanne went a little pale under her makeup.

"She's passed it to someone," she hissed to the security guard. "Find out who. Quickly!"

"How do you suggest I do that, Suzanne?" the guard inquired mildly. He looked around at the chattering people milling around the plaza.

Suzanne's eyes narrowed as she glanced in my direction. "These rabbit creatures were everywhere in the crowd before," she said. "And I'm sure this short one has been watching the shop. She's hardly moved from this spot."

Then she had another thought. She pointed at Tom. "Yesterday, the tall one playing the fool over there with the children was hanging around that criminal they call The Wolf. Make what you like of that!"

"I haven't been spying on your shop!" I burst out. My voice sounded strange, echoing inside the rabbit head. "I've just been doing my job — handing out leaflets. And Tom's done nothing, either."

"I want this rabbit searched," cried Suzanne. "And the other one. In fact, I want all the rabbits searched. Hurry — before they get away!"

The security guard sighed heavily. "Where would they go, Suzanne?" he asked. "Anyway, we'll leave the searching to the police. They'll be here any minute. And in the meantime, let's all keep our voices down. People are staring."

He beckoned to Liz, Tom, Nick, and Elmo, who were standing together by the INFORMATION sign. They hurried toward us.

I looked around the plaza. The janitor was leaning on his broom, scowling ferociously. Shopkeepers were at their doors, looking out. Disappointed-looking tourists were milling around, starting to leave. The opal-shopping expedition had come to an abrupt halt.

12

The trap

Of course, the police didn't find anything on any of us. But I had a feeling they weren't quite satisfied. They asked a lot of questions. And they were particularly interested in Tom and me.

When they finally let us leave, we hurried back to the Gingerbread House kitchen to talk. Mrs. Crumb spun around as we came in.

"What on earth happened?" she demanded. "What did the police want with you?"

Beside me, Tom shrugged. "The cops seem to think that little woman in glasses passed a ring she stole to one of us. We got searched."

"It's so ridiculous!" exclaimed Liz. "As if teenage kids would be involved."

"Why not?" Elmo put in slowly. "Dad says the cops are sure that The Wolf uses all sorts of people to do his dirty work."

I turned to him. "You think The Wolf's behind this?" I asked.

He shrugged. "Could be," he said. "He was here yesterday, wasn't he? He hung around the opal shop for a while, too. He could have been checking out the place."

"He also hung around the pharmacy, the men's shop, the bookshop, and the Gingerbread House," I pointed out. "Who knows what he was doing? He might just have been shopping. Didn't you say he often comes to the mall?"

"Yeah," Elmo agreed.

"The Wolf?" frowned Mrs. Crumb. "The Wolf? Is this a joke?"

Nick shook his head. "He's a criminal," he said. "He was here yesterday."

"A very big, fat man with bushy eyebrows," said Tom. He went to the storeroom and brought back the sketchbook from his bag. He flicked open the pages.

"There," he said, pointing. "I did this last night."

Mrs. Crumb looked at the sketch. Her face changed. "I know him," she exclaimed. "He comes in all the time. But he's never done anything unusual here. Never once."

"He doesn't do anything himself," said Elmo. "He gets other people to do it for him. He just organizes. The cops have probably been watching this place like they watch everywhere else he goes. Maybe that's why they were so ready to suspect us about the opal business."

Mrs. Crumb's face flushed with anger.

There was a scrabbling knock on the door that led out to the shop. Mrs. Crumb looked startled. She went to the door, slid the bolt, and pulled it open a little.

Richelle's flushed face appeared in the gap. Her big blue eyes stared at the rest of us resentfully. She obviously thought we were having a relaxing time while she slaved away.

"It's nearly noon, Mrs. Crumb," she said in a high-pitched

voice. "You said I should call you then. And there are lots and lots of people in the shop. And I'm getting very hot."

Mrs. Crumb looked flustered. "Ah, yes, Richelle," she said. "I'll be there in five minutes. I'll just get the muffins out of the oven." She glanced at us. "I suppose you want something to eat?" she said.

"A muffin or two will be fine," Tom suggested hopefully. But Mrs. Crumb didn't take any notice.

"Richelle will bring you some nut clusters," she said crisply. "We have more of those left than anything else, and they'll give you energy to go back to work."

"I'd set my heart on muffins," Tom complained under his breath. "Who needs nuts?"

I noticed, though, that he managed to eat three nut clusters in quick succession after Richelle brought them. I had one, too. I guess it gave me energy. But it didn't make going back to work any easier. Not at all.

❖

By two o'clock I was sick and tired of handing out leaflets. I was also sick and tired of being stared at by the opal shop people, the janitor, and the other shopkeepers. None of the looks were friendly. Even Mr. Melk, the pharmacist, had stopped waving and smiling. I think Suzanne had told everyone about her suspicions of us. It was irritating, silly, and unfair.

In half an hour, I'll be free to go, I said to myself. *I'll get home as fast as I can. Then I'll try to see Mom between patients. She won't mind just this once. I'll tell her what I've decided about going to*

Sydney. Then it will be done, finished with. No turning back. No more thinking and wondering what to do. No more questions.

The plan made me feel better. So the last thing I wanted was to see Darren Henshaw and Nutley Frean come grinning and slouching off the escalator, followed closely by two rabbits who must have been Liz and Nick. *More trouble,* I thought crossly. I didn't *want* any more trouble.

But I didn't have any choice.

Elmo and Tom came to join us, and we watched Darren and Nutley stroll, hands in pockets, toward the Gingerbread House.

"We'd better get over there," whispered Nick. "Tell Mrs. Crumb and Richelle. Make sure those goons don't plant anything else."

"At least the lunch rush is over," Liz said to me as I shuffled along, trying to keep up with her. "It should be easy to keep an eye on them if the shop's not too full."

I didn't say anything. She turned her rabbit head so that she could look at me. "Sunny, are you all right?" she asked.

"Why are you always asking me if I'm all right lately?" I snapped. My head buzzed with things I wanted to say but couldn't.

Darren and Nutley were hanging around outside the shop, pretending to look in the window as we passed them. They sneered at us, and flicked Tom's tail, but didn't say anything.

We went around to the back door. It was locked. Nick rapped urgently, and, in a moment, it was flung open. Warm, delicious-smelling air gusted into our faces. Mrs. Crumb peered out at us and frowned.

"It's not two-thirty yet," she accused. "What are you doing here? I'm terribly busy."

"Darren and Nutley are out front," gasped Liz, pulling off her rabbit head. "We came to tell you . . ."

Mrs. Crumb's face changed. "Ah!" she breathed. "I didn't think they'd have the nerve to go into the shop. I thought they'd try the kitchen again, if they came, so I kept the door shut."

"Is Richelle serving on her own?" Nick demanded. "Because you can't rely on her to notice anything —"

"Nick means," Liz rushed in, shooting him a furious glance, "that Richelle will be concentrating on the customers, and —"

Mrs. Crumb's mouth twitched. "I know exactly what he means, thank you, Liz," she said. She looked at her watch and nodded.

"I just have time," she said. "I'll deal with them now. Shouldn't take too long. Come in, kids. And lock the door behind you."

She opened the oven door, nodded, and pulled out a pan of big, fluffy muffins. She quickly arranged them on a cooling rack on the workbench, next to other racks of muffins already sitting there. I saw that she'd chalked MUFFINS on the little blackboard that she used as her SPECIALS sign, and thought again how efficient she was.

Tom moaned softly. "Chocolate, blueberry, chocolate chip," he murmured. "And what's that new batch? Apple and date, maybe? Oh, joy! Oh, bliss!"

Mrs. Crumb spun around. "These aren't to be touched!" she warned him, shaking her bony finger. "Do you understand?"

"Yes, Mrs. Crumb," said Tom meekly.

"I've counted them," she added sternly. "But just in case

you're tempted, you had better all come with me. It could help, anyway. As long" — she fixed us all with her cold eyes — "as long as you say nothing to them or to me, absolutely nothing, whatever happens. Just stand and watch. Do you understand?"

"What about Richelle?" asked Liz.

Mrs. Crumb smiled. "Ah, Richelle won't be a problem. Anything she says or does can only help. Now. Put on your heads! And leave them on."

Liz snickered. I must admit it did sound funny. But Mrs. Crumb didn't smile again. We all put our rabbit heads back on and followed her into the shop.

Richelle was staring out the front windows, ignoring Darren and Nutley, who were prowling around the side shelves, no doubt looking for good places to plant whatever they'd brought with them this time. There were no other customers.

As we filed in, Richelle looked around. Darren and Nutley did, too, and they grinned and nudged each other.

"Richelle, why are you just standing there?" hissed Liz as soon as she was close enough. "Those jerks could be doing *anything*!"

Richelle tossed her head. "They were *awful* to me when they came in," she said sulkily. "So I decided it was best to just ignore them."

"*What* a good idea," said Tom. She glared at him.

"Shhhh," muttered Liz. "We're supposed to keep quiet."

Mrs. Crumb strode over to Darren and Nutley.

"May I help you, boys?" she asked sweetly.

They looked at each other and smirked.

"No, thanks," said Darren. "Seeing as you haven't got any of your famous raisin-bran muffins left. They're my favorites."

Nutley Frean nudged him in the ribs. "Popular today, were they?" he said.

Darren snorted with laughter.

Mrs. Crumb's eyes were like cold stones. Now, I thought, she knew for sure that they put the flies into the muffin batter. They wouldn't have talked like that otherwise. And, of course, they didn't realize that the cakes were never baked and sold.

"I'm sorry you're disappointed, boys," she said. "I'll tell you what. I've just taken another batch of muffins out of the oven. A new recipe I'm trying. How about testing some for me? No charge."

"Hey!" Tom protested under his breath. "That's not fair!"

"Shhh," I whispered, watching Darren's eyes light up with greed.

Smiling sweetly, Mrs. Crumb went into the kitchen.

"She's sick of you, isn't she?" Darren snickered at us. "Now she's buttering us up so we'll take over your job when she fires you."

We stared at him in silence.

Mrs. Crumb reappeared with a basket full of muffins.

"Oh, no," breathed Tom, next to me. "The apple-and-date ones. I really wanted to try those."

I pushed against him, to shut him up.

"Come along, boys." Mrs. Crumb smiled and beckoned. My blood ran cold. Darren and Nutley deserved everything they got, but . . .

The two Work Demons leaped over to where Mrs. Crumb was standing. "Sit down," she said, pointing to the Hansel and Gretel stools by the wall and holding out the muffins. "Take the weight off your feet."

They sat down, took a muffin each, and started eating. Mrs. Crumb stepped back and in the same movement pulled the barred door into place. The padlock snapped shut under her fingers. The Work Demons were firmly caged.

13

Revenge is sweet

Nutley jumped up, startled. But Darren took another huge bite of his warm muffin and sneered at Mrs. Crumb. "Sit down," he snarled to his friend. "Finish your muffin. The old witch is on to us, apparently. So she's trying to scare us now. Thinks we're pre-schoolers."

Mrs. Crumb smiled again. "Richelle, please lock the front door," she called, without taking her eyes off the Work Demons. "Turn off the main light. And turn the sign around. We don't want to be disturbed."

Richelle did as she was told, locking the door and turning the OPEN sign around so that it read CLOSED. Then she switched off the main light. Now the shop was dim, lit only by the light coming in from outside.

I looked back at the caged Work Demons. Darren was sitting back, with his legs crossed. He stuffed the last of his muffin into his mouth and reached for another one. He didn't look worried.

Nutley was still chewing, but as I watched, a strange, puzzled expression crossed his face. He wrinkled his nose.

Then, suddenly, he pulled his half-eaten muffin away from his mouth and looked at it.

He screamed — a strange, high-pitched scream — and threw it to the ground.

"What's your problem?" snarled Darren. He was obviously getting a bit rattled himself now. But he bit into his second muffin defiantly.

Nutley was spitting and shaking. Crumbs were spraying everywhere. He panted and stammered, pointing to the muffin lying on the floor.

Darren looked at it. We all looked at it, straining our eyes in the dimness. From the pale gold cake stuck something ragged and brown. A date, I thought. And then I looked more closely —

My stomach lurched. I heard Liz make a stifled, choking sound.

"It's a cockroach," sputtered Nutley. "I-I've eaten some of it. Oh, no. No!"

Darren went white and clapped his hand over his mouth.

"You ate yours," squealed Nutley. "You ate the whole thing."

"Don't you like your muffins, boys?" smiled Mrs. Crumb, bending forward. Her nose almost met her chin. Her cold eyes glittered in her shadowed face. "Not tasty enough for you? I'm so sorry, but I could only put one cockroach into each. They were such big ones, you see."

Nutley shrank back. "You're crazy," he whimpered. "You've poisoned me. I'll get some really bad disease."

"Probably," agreed Mrs. Crumb calmly. "The cockroaches I used were some of the ones Darren brought into the kitchen earlier today. Who knows where they'd been? But you're better off than Darren, aren't you? He ate all his muffin. Cockroach and all. And now he's going to eat another one."

Darren was heaving and sweating. Suddenly, he threw away the muffin he was holding, flung himself at the bars of the cage, stuck his hands through, and began fighting and fumbling with the padlock.

Quick as a striking snake, Mrs. Crumb grabbed his hands in one of hers and twisted them, pulling so that Darren's face was pulled against the bars of the cage. He struggled against her grip, but couldn't break it. Her hand must have been like iron.

She picked up the muffin he had thrown away and held it up to his mouth. He tried to turn away, but he couldn't. He showed the whites of his eyes and began to whimper.

"Eat your muffin, Darren," said Mrs. Crumb. "It's lovely and fresh. Apple. With a crunchy, chewy surprise center. Made especially for you."

Tom swore under his breath. Liz was panting. "She can't make them eat cockroaches," she whispered in agony. "She can't!"

"Why not?" said Richelle, watching the scene with calm satisfaction. "They nearly made other people eat flies."

Mrs. Crumb was a better judge of people than I'd thought. She'd known how Richelle would react to this. We needed masks to hide our faces. Richelle didn't.

Nutley was sobbing and choking on the floor. "Please let us go!" he howled. "Please!"

I felt Liz grip my arm.

Mrs. Crumb raised her eyebrows. In the dim light she looked as mad and evil and witchy as anything in your worst nightmare.

"Oh, I can't possibly let you go," she said. "You're trying to close down my shop. Like you closed down Burger Joe's."

She smiled. "Sadly, boys, I really think you should disappear," she said softly. "And I was thinking. I was thinking that after you've eaten your muffins, right down to the last crumb, I could take you into the kitchen. I've got some big, heavy-duty pots there. And a nice, warm oven. And dozens of meat recipes. That should solve my problem nicely."

Nutley howled. "You're crazy!" he bawled. "Darren, she's crazy. She's going to eat us!"

Darren fought for control. "She's bluffing!" he said. "She can't do anything to us. Moysten and the others are watching, you stupid-head."

Mrs. Crumb grinned evilly, showing all her big white teeth. "You don't understand, do you, boys?" she cackled, looking over at us, standing silently behind the counter, five grinning white rabbits and a calm-faced Richelle.

"You didn't know who you were dealing with when you tangled with me," she went on, her voice low. "I have ways . . . of ensuring my safety. Nobody will remember anything about this, afterward. They won't even remember having seen you in the shop. I assure you."

Darren licked his lips. "Look, we'll leave you alone," he said. "We promise."

"Think I'd trust your promises, boy?" snarled Mrs. Crumb. "Think I'm stupid? Now . . ." She pushed the muffin against his mouth. "You just —"

"No! Please!" shouted Nutley. "Please! We'll do anything!

Don't make us eat cockroaches. Don't cook us up. Just let us out. I want to go home. I feel sick. Really sick."

Mrs. Crumb seemed to think for a moment. "Will you sign this?" she asked, after a moment.

She pulled a folded paper from her pocket, still holding Darren's hands in that terrible grip. She read the writing on the paper aloud.

"To Whom It May Concern: We admit that we planted dead cockroaches in Burger Joe's shop, sprayed the kitchen benches with dirty oil, and put bad meat in his refrigerator. We also put a dead mouse and cockroaches in the Gingerbread House, and put flies in a bowl of muffin batter."

Mrs. Crumb raised her eyebrows. "Well?" she said.

"I'll sign it," whimpered Nutley, clutching his stomach. "Hand it over."

She passed it through the bars of the cage and gave him a pen. He signed his name.

"Now Darren," she said.

She released Darren's hands. He snatched at the paper and signed it. Then he handed it back to her, quickly pulling his hand away afterward, in case she grabbed him again.

"Thank you," she said, folding the paper and putting it back into her pocket. "Now, I'm going to give this to the mall management. That will settle your debt here for a while. But I want to tell you something else, just from me."

She pushed her face close to the bars of the cage. "I never want to see you again," she hissed. "If I do, you'll regret it. I am quite capable of anything. Anything at all. Do you understand?"

They nodded, struck dumb.

So were we. Mrs. Crumb was very scary at that moment.

She lifted the key from its hook on the wall and unlocked the padlock. The cage door slid open. Nutley and Darren stumbled out and made for the front door.

"Open it for them, please," said Mrs. Crumb.

Richelle did as she asked. And in a moment, the two Work Demons had scuttled out of the Gingerbread House, without looking back.

"Well . . . that's that," said Mrs. Crumb, in a pleased voice. She strode to the door, flipped over the sign to read OPEN, and switched on the light.

"Now we can get back to work," she added.

We all just stared at her.

She laughed. "What's the problem?" she said. "Surely, you know that bullies are the worst cowards of all. And I haven't played the witch for all this time for nothing. Get out of those silly suits and go home. I'll see you in the morning."

"We'll clean up a bit for you," Tom said. His eyes were popping. "It's the least we can do."

I looked at my watch. I wanted to help. I decided my talk with Mom could wait a half an hour or so.

"Well, that would be nice," Mrs. Crumb said briskly. "And maybe Richelle could go on serving for a while. That will give me a chance to take this statement to the mall management and tell them what's been going on here."

She strode out of the shop, smiling graciously at a couple of customers who were coming in.

"We haven't got much to sell, actually," whispered Richelle

as the customers looked around the shelves. "With Julie away, the stock's practically gone."

"Is that all you can say?" exploded Liz. "Have you ever seen *anything* like that? The woman's terrifying! And she baked a whole batch of muffins with *cockroaches* in them."

Richelle shrugged. "Only the apple-and-date ones," she said. "I'm sure the others are OK."

"Richelle, she said she'd make Darren and Nutley into her dinner," breathed Liz.

"But she was just scaring them, wasn't she? She wouldn't really have done it," Elmo said.

"She sounded very sincere to me," Tom put in.

"Of course, she wouldn't have done it," sneered Nick. "Don't be ridiculous."

I agreed with Nick. I think.

14

The fast lane

Richelle bustled around behind the counter while we swept up the muffin crumbs and washed the floor. We'd taken off our heads. After what we'd been through, customers seeing us headless seemed the least of our worries.

Liz closed her eyes as she swept Nutley's half-finished muffin into a piece of newspaper.

"Is it really a cockroach?" whispered Nick.

"Beats me," she said, shuddering. "Nutley certainly thought it was, anyway. And I'm not going to look any more closely than I have to."

The customers left the shop with the last of the chocolate éclairs. Elmo looked through the open door into the plaza.

"There are lots of people out there," he said. "We'd better finish up here quickly and go back out to the kitchen. We're only half dressed."

Then he leaned forward, his eyes alight. "The Wolf's back!" he exclaimed. "He's over there by the pharmacy."

"Is the policeman following him again?" I asked.

"No . . . I can't see him," Elmo said. "Boy, The Wolf's got a lot of nerve. After that opal theft this morning, you'd think he'd keep away for a while."

Playing games, I thought. *He can't resist it.*

We all crowded to the door to look. Except for Richelle, who had brought Mrs. Crumb's SPECIALS blackboard from the kitchen and was sticking it in the window.

"Hey, Sunny," exclaimed Liz. "There's your dad. Look, see? Just getting off the escalator."

I looked, and my stomach turned over. Dad must be coming to see me.

Richelle bustled to the kitchen and came back with a rack of chocolate muffins.

Liz noticed what she was doing for the first time. "Richelle, you can't sell those!" she cried.

Richelle flicked back her hair and looked bored. "Liz, I'm in charge here," she said. "And you heard Mrs. Crumb say only one pan of muffins was for Darren and Nutley. I've left them. The apple-and- . . . um . . . date ones. They're still quite hot, anyway. These chocolate ones are quite cold. She must have made them earlier. Before lunch, probably. We've been so busy, she just forgot to bring them out."

Two women stopped outside the shop, saw the sign, and came in. They bought four muffins each and handed them out to their kids as they went back out to the plaza.

We watched anxiously through the windows as the kids chewed away happily. Nothing happened. The muffins seemed fine. We all breathed a sigh of relief.

Richelle looked pleased. "Mrs. Crumb relies on me to use my initiative," she said smugly.

Tom groaned. "Why don't you use your initiative and give me a muffin, then?" he said.

I was hardly listening. I was watching my father cross the plaza. He arrived at the Gingerbread House and walked in, smiling broadly.

When he saw me and the others, he burst out laughing.

"Sorry," he said finally, wiping his eyes. "You just look . . . crazy! And, boy, this place! What an amazing coincidence, eh, Sunny?"

I was confused. I wanted to ask him what he meant, but already he was moving forward, hand outstretched, wanting to be introduced to everyone.

He'd met Liz before, but I introduced him to the others. I could see that they were very interested in him, and felt a mixture of pride and embarrassment. It was so strange, having a tennis star for a father.

But there was something else, of course. I knew Dad was bound to say something about me going to Australia with him. He wasn't like Mom. He wouldn't wait for a sign from me that I'd told them.

I was right. "So how do you feel about Sunny taking off?" he said to Liz. "Guess you'll miss her."

Liz's jaw dropped. Her eyes widened. She turned to me, her face full of questions.

My lips felt stiff. "I'm going to Sydney, Australia, to live with Dad for a while," I said flatly.

Liz clapped her hand to her mouth.

"Sunny!" exclaimed Tom. "Sunny, why didn't you say anything?"

There was dead silence in the shop.

I felt myself blushing. I looked around at their faces and found myself shocked by what I saw there. They all looked terribly upset. Elmo was pink and serious. Nick was frowning. Tom's face was wrinkled and anxious. And even Richelle was leaning across the counter looking concerned.

I hadn't been prepared for this.

Dad put his arm around my shoulders. "It's a big chance for Sunny, guys," he said. "She'll get the best coaching around. She deserves it, don't you think?"

Tom was the first to recover. He forced a smile. "Oh, yes!" he said. "'Course she does." He punched the air at me. "Sunny, that's great!" he said.

The others chimed in with congratulations, even Liz.

Then there was another one of those silences.

"When are you leaving?" asked Elmo.

"On Friday," I said. I heard Liz gasp, but I couldn't look at her.

"Well, the fact is, Sunny, that's why I'm here," my father said. "Plans have changed. We're leaving tonight."

"Tonight?" I gasped. "But-but I can't go tonight. I've got this job, for a start. Till the end of the week."

Dad laughed. "That can't be helped, sweetie. The job'll have to take care of itself. An old friend called this morning from Melbourne. He's just done a deal to set up a tennis clinic there. Real big, resort stuff. And he wants me there. For six months or so, to help him get started. But I've got to get there in twenty-four hours."

I blinked. Things were going too quickly for me. "Melbourne? I-I thought we were going to Sydney," I stammered.

"We *were* going to Sydney," grinned Dad. "But now that this has come up, I can't pass on it. That's life in the fast lane, Sunny. You go where the chances are. Where the big bucks are, too. Right, guys?"

He looked around at the others. They nodded.

"Right!" said Nick. It was what he always said himself, I remembered. But somehow he didn't sound so enthusiastic at the moment.

"We'll tell Mrs. Crumb, Sunny," said Liz in a small voice. "Don't worry. It'll be fine."

Dad squeezed my shoulder. "Well, why don't you get that crazy rabbit suit off, sweetie, and we'll go. My car's in a no-parking zone. You need to talk to your mother and pack. We've only got a few hours. Don't want to miss the plane!"

I went into the kitchen and started pulling off my suit. I felt so spaced out. Everything seemed unreal. I hung up the suit in the storeroom next to Richelle's, grabbed my bag, and went back out into the shop.

Richelle was selling Dad two muffins. She was smiling and tossing her hair back. She was enjoying this job much more than she'd enjoyed being a rabbit. *She'd only worn her suit for one day so far*, I thought. But she'd have to wear it again tomorrow, because Julie would be back working for Mrs. Crumb then for sure.

But there wouldn't be six rabbits out in the plaza anymore. I'd be gone.

I rubbed my eyes. Something was nibbling away at the edge of my mind. Something I couldn't quite catch and look at up close.

I shook my head impatiently.

"Ready, Sunny?" Dad was leaning against the counter, swinging his bag of muffins and smiling at me. He looked relaxed, confident, very alive.

I turned to Liz. Her eyes were full of tears.

"I'll write," I said. "I'll . . . miss you. I'm sorry I didn't . . . tell you." Suddenly, to my horror, I felt my throat tighten. I couldn't go on.

Liz hugged me hard. "It's all right," she whispered. "I know . . . how you are. And I would have made a fuss. You wouldn't like that." Her voice began to tremble. "I hope . . . you'll be very happy, Sunny."

She let me go and I went around and hugged the others good-bye, too. Even Richelle. She smelled of makeup, shampoo, perfume, and muffins.

Dad put his arm around me. We walked to the door. We waved. And we left the shop.

15

Memories

I hesitated outside for a moment. Everything in the plaza was the same. The crabby janitor was emptying a garbage can. Mr. Melk was standing by his door. Kids chased one another around the INFORMATION sign.

My mind was a blank. So, somehow, I was hardly shocked at all when I realized that The Wolf was right beside me, looking in the window of the Gingerbread House.

He scowled at us under his bushy eyebrows. Then he pushed past and lumbered into the shop. I looked around for his follower. As Elmo had said, the skinny policeman wasn't anywhere to be seen, but a tall redheaded man pretending to read a newspaper outside the bookstore was probably his replacement, I thought.

Dad looked after The Wolf. "That's one big guy," he said.

I nodded. "He's a criminal," I said. "Big-time."

We started walking across the plaza.

Dad was staring at me. "For real?" he asked. "How do you know? And what's a guy like that doing here? Nothing ever happens in Raven Hill."

"Lots of things happen in Raven Hill," I said, thinking back. "You'd be surprised."

Mrs. Crumb met us at the top of the escalator. She nodded to Dad and smiled at me. "See you tomorrow, Sunny," she said.

"Oh — I'm sorry," I said awkwardly. "But I've just found out I have to go away. To Australia. Tonight."

Mrs. Crumb's face fell into a frown. "Well, that's a bit awkward," she said.

"Can't be helped, though," Dad said cheerfully. "These things happen."

She crossly opened her mouth to say something, and then her expression changed. She was looking over my shoulder, across the plaza. "What . . . ?" she muttered to herself.

I twisted around to see what had caught her attention. It was The Wolf, shouldering his way out of the Gingerbread House door with a bulging paper bag in his hand.

"Well, good-bye," muttered Mrs. Crumb. She began making for her shop as fast as she could, but walking at an angle, so she wouldn't have to meet The Wolf on the way. She strode past the grumpy janitor, who was now sweeping up litter from around the garbage can, and nearly tripped on his broom. He snarled at her, but she didn't look back.

"Let's get out of here," I said, and stepped onto the escalator.

We were nearly down to the ground floor when I remembered something I'd wanted to ask.

"What did you mean before, when you said it was a strange coincidence, me working at the Gingerbread House?" I said.

Dad looked at me in surprise. "Well, you know, honey," he said. "'Hansel and Gretel.' The book."

"What book?" I was honestly bewildered.

"The book of fairy tales," Dad said. "The big one, with all the pictures. You must remember it. I used to read it to you just about every night."

I blinked at him as I stepped off the escalator. "I had forgotten," I said slowly. "But now . . . I'm starting to remember. It was a big blue book."

"That's right," Dad said as he led me toward the mall entrance. "A big blue book. It had everything — 'Little Red Riding Hood,' 'Goldilocks and the Three Bears,' 'Sleeping Beauty' — all those. But 'Hansel and Gretel' was your favorite. I must have read that thing fifty times."

I half closed my eyes. Slowly, my mind filled with pictures. Vividly colored pictures on shiny paper. Little Red Riding Hood and the wolf. Goldilocks being frightened by the bears. Sleeping Beauty lying in her bed in a crown and a white dress. And . . .

"The Gingerbread House!" I gasped. "The house in the picture — it looked just like the shop upstairs!"

My heart was beating like a mad drum. The picture grew stronger and stronger in my mind. Bright colors on shiny paper. Candy-cane posts, toffee-colored front door, sugar-frosted windows. And beckoning from the door was the grinning witch.

I clutched my chest.

We walked out of the mall. There was the car Dad had rented, pulled up right at the entrance. A parking ticket was stuck under the windshield wiper. Dad laughed and stuck it in his pocket. He passed me the bag of muffins and felt for his keys.

"The old girl must have seen the same book," he said. "Copied the design for her shop. Did it well, didn't she?" He found his keys and went around to the driver's side of the car to open the door.

The memories were getting clearer and clearer now. I was breathing hard. My hands were slippery with sweat.

Dad slipped into the driver's seat and opened the passenger door for me. "Hop in," he said. Then he noticed, I guess, that I was looking strange. "What's the matter, honey?" he asked.

I licked my lips. "The book," I said. "I was reading the book, looking at the pictures, the night you . . . left us."

He shrugged. "Probably," he said. "You looked at it all the time. Funny kid. Liked being scared, I guess. So what?"

I didn't answer. Suddenly, I was four years old again. I was sitting in my bed, waiting for Dad to come and read me "Hansel and Gretel." There was shouting downstairs, but I was trying not to listen to it. Quite often lately, there was shouting in the house. I always tried to shut it out. I didn't understand it, and it worried me.

The big blue book was open on my knees. The picture of the Gingerbread House glowed on its shiny paper. The witch beckoned.

Then Dad was at the door. It was Daddy, of course, in those days. My daddy, whom I loved more than anything or anyone else in the world. He came over to the bed and put his arms around me.

"Sunny, little honey, I came to say good-bye," he said to me.

I thought he was just going out, and I was angry. I wanted him to read to me.

"I'm going away," he said. "You're too little to understand, but I can't stay here anymore. I've stayed too long already. It's a backwater town. It's killing me. Kids — house — all that. And in Australia I can . . ."

His voice went on and on. I just stared at my book, while my world fell apart. The house in the picture glowed like an evil thing. Still, the witch beckoned, grinning.

"I'll come back and visit," Dad was saying. But that didn't mean anything to me. All I knew was that he was going to leave me. Just like Hansel and Gretel's father left them, lost in the forest . . .

Slowly, I came back to the present. I looked down at Dad's face as he peered up from the open car door at me. "I'd forgotten it all," I whispered. "But now I remember."

"Well, that's fine, sweetie," he said, looking puzzled. "Now if you've finished your trip down memory lane, can we go?" He sat back up in his seat and started the car engine. "Or are you missing your life as a white rabbit already?" he shouted over the noise. "I wouldn't. There are plenty up there without you. And who could tell the difference?"

I blinked at him. And without warning, the thing that had been drifting at the corner of my mind suddenly moved into the center of it and came into focus. I gripped the car door. Hard.

"Dad," I said urgently. "Dad, I have to go back. To the Gingerbread House. I have to see the gang. Tell them something. It's important."

His forehead puckered in irritation. "Oh, c'mon, honey," he said. "There's no time. Listen, you don't owe those friends of yours a thing. That's all over. They're ancient history now. Right?"

I shook my head. Wrong.

"Sunny, this isn't like you," he said, frowning and revving the engine.

You wouldn't know, I thought. *You wouldn't know what I am like.*

"I have to go back," I repeated stubbornly.

He shook his head in frustration. "You do what you like, then," he said angrily. "I've got to keep moving. And I'll be catching that plane at seven with you or without you. OK?"

I nodded, turned, and ran back into the mall. By the time I'd reached the escalators, I'd forgotten all about him.

16

Terror

The Gingerbread House was closed and shuttered, so I ran around to the back. I could hear the gang talking in the kitchen. The door was half open and I peeped in.

Liz squealed when she saw me and pulled me inside.

"Didn't you like Australia?" grinned Tom.

But I didn't have time for jokes.

"Listen," I said. "I came back to tell you something. I've just realized —" Then I stopped and looked around.

"Where's Mrs. Crumb?" I asked.

Nick snorted. "Running around the mall like a hen with its head cut off," he said. "Looking for people who bought muffins. Seems Richelle made a big mistake, selling them."

Richelle sniffed. For the first time, I noticed that her eyes were red and puffy. "She needn't have screamed at me like that," she muttered. "I was only trying to help. And I only sold one tray. But how am I supposed to remember who bought them?"

"Well," said Tom wickedly, "you sold two to The Wolf. I remember that. And didn't those women buy four each?"

"And I've got two," I said, looking down at the paper bag

I still had clutched in my hand. "What's supposed to be in this batch? Flies? Snails? Baby mice?"

Richelle shuddered. "I don't know," she said. "All I know is, Mrs. Crumb went nuts, and then rushed off, and —"

"But listen, Sunny," Liz interrupted. "What did you have to tell us?"

I took a deep breath. "Listen," I said. "This morning, when the opal was stolen — there were too many rabbits."

"What?" Nick was staring at me. They all were.

"Too many rabbits," I repeated. "It's been nibbling away at me all afternoon, and finally, I've realized why."

"Why, then?" asked Elmo. "Go on."

"Well," I said, "there was one rabbit near the INFORMA-TION sign."

Tom bowed.

"And there was another one in the middle of the crowd," I went on.

"That was me, I think," said Elmo.

"Well, two more rabbits were coming up the escalator with the tourists —"

"You and me," Nick put in, looking at Liz.

I nodded. "So —" I looked around at the circle of puzzled faces. "So who was the sixth rabbit? The one I saw on the first floor, moving into the crowd from the side?"

They hesitated. "Not Richelle," said Nick slowly. "Because Richelle was serving in the shop."

"That's right," I said. "So —"

"So someone else was in the plaza, wearing Richelle's rabbit suit, pretending to be one of us," murmured Elmo, following it through. "They took the opal from that woman with glasses and slipped away again in the crowd. Then they must have come back here, taken off the suit —"

"And, of course," I said, "there's only one person who —"

Suddenly, I paused. I had heard a sound from the shop. A tiny noise, like a floorboard creaking under the weight of someone's foot. Right behind the door. Someone was listening to us. The hair stood up on the back of my neck.

I quickly ran through the last few minutes of our conversation in my mind. Only one female voice. Mine. But it could have been Liz's, as far as the listener was concerned. There was no reason to think otherwise, since I was supposed to be gone.

I put my fingers to my lips and backed away toward the storeroom. The others stared after me.

"What are you doing?" began Richelle crossly.

And then the door swung open, and Mrs. Crumb was standing there. She beckoned. But this time she wasn't smiling. And she had a gun in her hand.

❂

I crept out of the storeroom and stood behind the open swing door, hardly daring to breathe. I couldn't get out of the kitchen to go for help. Mrs. Crumb had locked the back door before she put the others into the cage. And she had her keys with her.

I thanked my lucky stars that she didn't realize I'd come back. As I'd hoped, she thought it was Liz she'd heard talking to the others.

She was growling at them now as she paced in front of the cage.

"I made a mistake with you kids, didn't I?" she snarled. "I chose you after I heard about that disaster at Burger Joe's. Suited me to have stupid, sloppy workers. I didn't want to hire kids who were too bright. They might notice what was going on. By the time I found out you weren't the dimwits I'd thought, it was too late to back out."

Well, that figures. I thought it was strange that a clever woman like Mrs. Crumb would be so bad at choosing people to help her out.

"You kids have been nothing but trouble for me from start to finish," Mrs. Crumb went on. She was breathing hard. It was obvious that she was very angry.

"First, those idiotic Work Demons nearly ruined everything because of you. Then you put me in danger by selling goods you were told not to touch. And to cap it all off, just now you —"

"It wasn't just now. We caught on to you ages ago," Tom broke in. "Long before Sunny left." His voice was shaking, but he went on, desperately trying to convince her.

"That's right. There was an extra rabbit, and it must have been you," Liz chimed in. "The kitchen doors were locked because you were supposed to be baking. No one else could have gotten into the storeroom. Sunny knows about it all. She's probably bringing the police right now. You'd better let us go."

Mrs. Crumb made an angry sound, as though she was growling between gritted teeth.

"Don't try to fool me," she spat. "You worked it out just a

minute ago. I heard you. And besides, I met your precious Sunny and her father on their way out of the mall. They obviously didn't know a thing. And that's lucky for her. She'll be in Australia soon. You'll be goners."

"Why hurt us? We don't need to say anything to the police." That was Liz's voice again. She was trying to sound calm and reasonable. "We hardly know anything, really, Mrs. Crumb. And who'd believe us? We're only kids."

Mrs. Crumb laughed. It was an ugly laugh, with no humor in it.

"The *police*?" she snarled. "Do you think I'm scared of *them*? You're an idiot, girl. What can the law do to me? A few years in jail, maybe? But how long do you think I'll last now, even in jail, when The Wolf thinks I've double-crossed him?"

"The Wolf!" gasped Elmo. And the name echoed in my head, too. The Wolf. Mrs. Crumb had been working for The Wolf.

And then, suddenly, I understood it all. All the little clues of the past two days fell into place: cream puffs; poor, silly Julie; Mrs. Crumb's absolute fury about the Work Demons; the rabbit suits; the SPECIALS sign; muffins that weren't to be sold. Everything.

I was still clutching the crumpled bag of muffins Dad had bought. I looked at it. My heart thumped. The whole tray of chocolate ones had been sold. Twelve muffins in all. And Mrs. Crumb was beside herself.

I thought it through. The Wolf had bought two of them, and he, apparently, was going to be angry. The two women had bought four each, and we'd watched their kids eat them with no problems. Dad had bought the other two.

So . . . I slipped my fingers into the bag, hoping against hope.

"What are you going to do with us?" chirped Liz.

"There's going to be a terrible tragedy, Liz," crooned Mrs. Crumb. "Afterward, people are going to say I lost my temper with you, just like I lost it with Darren and Nutley. I locked you in the cage, like I did with them."

She smiled. "They'll testify that I was crazy. They'll tell everything they know, when they hear the news. Five teenagers and an eccentric, middle-aged woman, tragically killed."

She sighed. "Boiling oil is so dangerous," she said. "In a small pot it can easily overflow and cause a fire. And what if the room were filled with gas? There'd be a terrible explosion, wouldn't there? A terrible explosion."

Richelle began to cry.

"You're crazy! You'll never get away with it!" shouted Nick. "You're trying to scare us."

That was what Darren Henshaw had said. But with a chill I realized that this time Mrs. Crumb wasn't acting. This time, the evil was real.

"Oh, no," cackled Mrs. Crumb. "I know exactly what I'm doing. With the arrangements I've made, there'll be nothing left of this place but rubble, a few twisted bars, and a bunch of charred bones. Yours. And by the stove, mine. Or what people will *think* are mine."

I heard a thump, and a dragging sound. I couldn't stand it. I held my breath and peeped around the door. Mrs. Crumb was dragging a sack from deep inside a gap under the counter. She tipped the sack out in front of the cage. A small heap of bones clattered to the floor. They looked real.

I heard the others gasp above Richelle's sobs.

"Ah, children, as you see, I've had this planned for a long, long time," crooned Mrs. Crumb. "Since The Wolf set me up here, as a matter of fact. My arrangements cost me a pretty penny. But as insurance, they were cheap at twice the price."

Her voice softened. I had to strain to hear it.

"Dealing with The Wolf, you never know when you might suddenly need to 'die' unexpectedly," she cackled. "I just didn't know there'd be cooked kiddies in the mix as well. Ah, well . . . time to put the oil on. Then I'll lock the back door and leave you. Bye-bye!"

She started for the kitchen. I shrank back against the wall, my hand still feeling around in my paper bag. Then, like the answer to a prayer, I felt something hard under my fingers. My whole body started to tingle. It was now or never.

17

Now or never

Mrs. Crumb strode through the swing door and went straight to the stove. She put her gun down on the counter. Then, humming to herself, she heaved a huge bottle of oil from underneath and filled a medium-size saucepan.

She set the pan on the stove, lit the gas, and turned it up high. Then she turned on all the other gas jets, too.

She meant what she said. She was planning to blow the shop sky-high and pretend she'd died in the explosion.

I could hear the others rattling the bars of the cage and calling out. But I knew no one would hear them. The front windows were already shuttered and locked. The front door was thick, and it was dead bolted, too. Once Mrs. Crumb left with her keys, locking the back door as well, we were trapped.

Mrs. Crumb went to the ovens, opened them, and turned on the gas. Her preparations were nearly complete.

I looked at the gun, lying black and deadly on the countertop. I calculated my chances of getting to it before she did. They were slim, I thought. And I knew better than to touch a loaded weapon, anyway.

No. I had to use the weapons I had. The fact that she didn't know I was there. The fact that I knew her weakness. Plus, the fact that, thanks to Dad, I had something she wanted.

In less than a minute, my first weapon paid off. Still humming, Mrs. Crumb left the stove and walked back into the shop.

I left my hiding place behind the door and ran toward the gun. I couldn't believe my eyes: It was a BB gun! I recognized it from the sporting goods store in the mall. I picked it up, anyway, and dropped it into the pan of heating oil.

Then I went and stood behind the swing door again, waiting for Mrs. Crumb to come back.

She soon did, carrying the pile of bones. She began arranging them on the floor by the stove.

She's the one who's stupid, I thought. *Those bones won't fool anyone. They'll know she tried to fake her own death.*

But that wouldn't help us.

That thought had just passed through my mind when Mrs. Crumb straightened up and noticed that the gun was missing.

She stared at the countertop where it had been and blinked her eyes. She looked all around the kitchen.

I couldn't give her time to look in the pan. It would only make her angrier. I stepped from behind the door. I held out what I had in my hand.

"Look, Mrs. Crumb," I said. "I found this ring in my muffin. Do you want it?"

I darted through the door into the shop. With a screech of rage she ran after me.

"Sunny!" screamed Liz as I ran past the cage and toward the counter.

Mrs. Crumb was after me. Her clawed hands stretched out in front of her as she ran. Her ugly face was twisted into a mask of rage.

But I wasn't scared of her now. The moment my father had made me remember that picture book, all my dread of Hazel Crumb and the Gingerbread House had fallen away. Now I was myself again. And Hazel — she was just a wicked woman who was a danger to me and my friends.

I dodged along behind the counter. With a grunt of satisfaction she followed me. She nearly had me. Nearly . . .

And then my hand had snaked out to pull the huge candy jars from the shelf, one by one. They were smashing on the ground in front of her, spilling their contents everywhere. Rainbow gum balls and toffees and jelly beans tumbled and rolled on the broken glass under Mrs. Crumb's flying feet, tripping her up and making her stumble. She finally fell flat on her face.

Then she was crawling to her feet, bruised, stumbling after me. Swearing and screaming.

"You little devil!" she shrilled. "Give me that ring! Give it to me!"

She was beside herself. She had completely lost her temper, as I'd planned. Her temper was her weakness. All she could think about was the ring I held in my hand. Her passport to safety from The Wolf.

I thundered back into the kitchen. It was full of gas now. The oil was simmering on the stove. Soon, it would come to a boil and overflow, and then the fire would start.

But she was after me. I didn't have time to stop. I was heading for the oven. The big, empty oven that hung open, belching out gas fumes.

I threw the ring into it. It disappeared, with a clatter, into the blackness. Then I turned off the oven.

With a howl, Mrs. Crumb sprang forward. She stuck her head and shoulders into the oven, scrabbling for the ring.

And then I slammed the door on her, as hard as I could. Just like Hansel did to the witch. She stiffened, groaned, and lay still. I had knocked her out cold.

I might have forgotten a lot of things.

But not my fairy tales.

❁

"So the Gingerbread House was The Wolf's post office," said Tom as we sat in Burger Joe's two days later. Thanks to Darren and Nutley's confession, Joe was back in business.

"When you think about it, it's obvious," Nick nodded, pushing away his plate. "He and his people would pass Mrs. Crumb things, like messages, or money, or in this case, an opal ring, while she was serving them. Then she'd put whatever it was into a muffin, and pass it on — to whomever gave the right password, I guess."

"She used the SPECIALS sign to signal that she was ready to pass over the goods," added Liz, with her mouth full. "She always served the specials herself, because she knew which cakes were the ones that had the goodies inside."

"The last thing she wanted was health inspectors looking at the food," I added. "That's why she was so *furious* about the Work Demons."

"She showed them, anyway," Richelle smiled contentedly.

Elmo sighed. "I was completely on the wrong track," he admitted. "I'd decided the janitor was the bad guy. The Wolf was always dropping garbage that he picked up. I was keeping a close eye on him."

"That could have been it, Elmo," Liz soothed. He nodded rather mournfully.

"You know, the Gingerbread House scheme could have gone on forever, if The Wolf hadn't gone after that opal ring," said Nick. "It was one thing to get that woman in the glasses to steal it for him. But he knew she'd never get out of the mall with it. So he invented the whole idea of the rabbit team to give Mrs. Crumb a way of taking it from her without anyone knowing."

He shook his head in puzzlement. "It was so dangerous. Why did he bother? The ring's valuable, but not worth risking the whole organization he'd built up, surely."

"He got too cocky," I said. "I watched him. He just loved teasing the police. He couldn't resist the idea of taking that ring in broad daylight, under their noses. Didn't you say he was a gambler?"

Elmo nodded.

We sat in silence for a moment. I knew everyone felt the same way I did. Tired out. Spaced out. A lot had happened to us in the past few days.

"Seconds, anyone?" Julie, wearing the red-checked apron and cap that Burger Joe had decided would give his waitresses class, beamed down at us. She, at least, was full of energy. Her new job suited her just fine.

"For free," she added. "Burger Joe says anything you want is on the house."

"Well, if that's the case . . ." beamed Tom, and started rattling off a whole new order.

"No wonder Mrs. Crumb was so upset with me when I sold the chocolate muffins," giggled Richelle. "She'd hidden the opal ring in one of them." She shook back her hair. "Boy, did I fool her!"

"Richelle!" barked Liz. "It almost got us killed!"

Richelle opened her big blue eyes. "Well, it didn't, did it?" she said. "And now that horrible Mrs. Crumb is in jail, and because she talked her head off when the police got her, so is the woman who stole the ring, and the awful Wolf man. And we got a reward from Exclusive Opals. Thanks to me."

"Thanks to you?" exploded Tom. "Thanks to Sunny, you mean. If she hadn't knocked out Crumb with the oven door, we'd be at our own funerals now, instead of eating hamburgers."

Richelle blinked at him. "Well, you *expect* Sunny to come through, don't you?" she said. "Sunny's reliable. That's what's so good about Sunny."

She squinted as she pulled her hair forward, checking it for split ends. "It's lucky Sunny isn't going to Australia after all," she yawned. "I don't know what we'd do without her."

"Richelle, you're a very deep thinker, you know that?" jeered Tom.

Liz put her arm around my shoulders. "I'm so glad you decided to stay, Sunny," she said.

I grinned. "So am I," I agreed.

And I meant it. I could have said to her: "Liz, I suddenly

realized how much you all meant to me. You, and everything else in my life here. I suddenly realized that my dad's lifestyle wouldn't suit me at all. Rushing around the world. Going after what he calls 'the big bucks.' Changing plans every two minutes. I suddenly realized that however much Dad loves me, in his way, and however charming and good-looking and funny he is, I could never rely on him. Like I could rely on my mom. Or you."

But, of course, I didn't say it. That's not my way. Just like it isn't my mother's way. When I told her, after the whole Gingerbread House thing was over and she had come to get me at the police station, that I wanted to stay with her, she didn't cry. She didn't gush or fuss. But she held me very close. And Penny, Cathy, Sarah, and Amy, who had all come with her, actually *cheered*. I had no idea they felt like that.

But I'll always know now. Just like I'll know that all the members of the Help-for-Hire gang really like having me around. Not just Liz, but Nick, Tom, and Elmo as well.

And even Richelle, apparently.

Now that's *really* saying something.

NIGHTMARE VACATION

EMILY RODDA'S
RAVEN HILL MYSTERIES

#4: DEEP SECRETS

◼SCHOLASTIC

...he Help-for-Hire team has definitely earned some time off. But when ...ey arrive at Aunt Vivien's mansion for a little R&R, two nasty caretakers ...t them to work with backbreaking chores, and Aunt Vivien is nowhere to ... seen. Their search for her leads them to a pitch-black well, which may ...ove to be a terrifying trap.

Welcome to Raven Hill. . .where danger means business.

◼**SCHOLASTIC**

EMILY RODDA'S DELTORA

Join the Quest into a Realm o

MONSTERS AND MAGI

Go to www.scholastic.com/deltoraquest to learn mo
about Deltora and its mysterious lands.

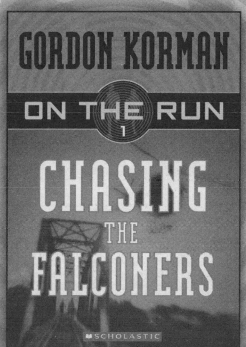